DEDICATIONS

For my daughter Yve
and my partner Maeve

fResh WateR

&
other stories

by

Neil Brosnan

ORIGINAL WRITING

978-1-907179-72-3

The stories listed below were first published in the following journals:

Fresh Water: Writers' Week, Listowel, Winners' anthology 2004

Good Intentions: Dunlavin Festival of Arts Anthology 2005

Driven: Splinters: 2008

Last Dance: Ireland's Own: 2006

A CIP catalogue for this book is available from the National Library.

Published by Original Writing Ltd., Dublin, 2010.

Printed by Cahill Printers Limited, Dublin.

ACKNOWLEDGEMENTS

My thanks to Mary and Billy Keane, Mickey and Maura MacConnell, John McGrath, Mary Kelly-Godley, Mike Gallagher, Marian Finan Hewitt, Tommy Frank O'Connor, Leland Bardwell and Noel King.

A very special thanks to Maeve O'Sullivan without whose support and encouragement this publication could not have come about.

Introduction

Neil Brosnan is a master of the short story.

There is a rhythm and a flow to his pieces that knits together the different seams and stitching as if by invisible mending.

Neil is an accomplished songwriter and this background in music shows itself in the cadence of his work.

Each story is a separate working but Neil's love of place and empathy with his fellow human beings are constant. The stories are essentially based on relationships and all the turbulence, love, trauma, drama and topsy-turviness that is bound up in how we interact with each.

But this is done in an understated way. Brosnan's tales are related without fanfare. The writing is open, honest and without too many big words. He has resisted showing off and the apparent simplicity of the telling masks the layers of meaning that stay with you afterwards. It is the aftertaste that makes his short stories truly memorable.

Many of Neil's tales have been published individually in different journals over the years. Some have won awards. Neil is a Listowel Writer's Week winner and now, after much persuasion, the songwriter has given us his greatest hits.

This is a beside the bed book. Take it up and it will put you to sleep! I mean this in the best possible way. The book is easy reading. Neil Brosnan takes us away from the here and now and we forget the daily grind yet, paradoxically, his stories are very much rooted in the not so simple world we live in.

Each story is a treat in itself. The collection – a treasure.

Billy Keane

CONTENTS

FRESH WATER

"Have you got a fishing rod?" Tony blinked, wondering what relevance fishing could have to his summer job as a hotel porter. The manager eyed him expectantly from across his desk, in the tiny office at the rear of reception.

"Yes, I've got one at home... someplace. I used to..."

"Good! You know the river, so?"

"Well, sort of..."

"If I wanted to catch a fish tomorrow, could you show me where to go?"

"I suppose so but the water is..." The boss was nodding impatiently.

"Right, so you'll act as guide for one of our guests tomorrow?"

"But the water..."

"It beats cleaning toilets!"

"What time?"

"Eight sharp. It's Mr. Shanahan, that American in two twenty-three. You needn't wear the white shirt."

"I could bring my wellies?" Tony suggested hopefully.

"Wear whatever you want!"

Locating the rod and reel was easy; they were still exactly where Tony's mother had stored them some five years before, beneath the rafters of the turf-shed. Unearthing the rest of his tackle proved more difficult. Tony's frantic campaign of rummaging through drawers, cupboards and rusting biscuit tins, drew the inevitable question from his father.

"What are you looking for?" A pair of enquiring eyes twinkled from above their reading lenses.

"Fishing gear, I thought I had more than this." Tony indicated the few spinners, hooks and other oddments resurrected from a variety of glory holes.

"What brought this on all of a sudden? You haven't been near the river in years."

1

"They want me to take a resident fishing tomorrow!"

"But there's no water. This is the driest summer for years. No one in his right mind would go near the river in its present state."

"He's an American!"

"Oh! Well, in that case, I wish you luck!" Tony resumed his quest to the accompaniment of rustling newspaper.

The hotel lobby was empty except for a mountainous figure whose meaty fingers ceased drumming the reception counter at Tony's punctual arrival.

"Mr Shanahan?" A pair of pale blue eyes appraised the speaker from beneath the brim of a feather-festooned bucket hat.

"Are you the bellboy?" The voice was deep but not unfriendly.

"I'm supposed to show you the river." Self-consciously, Tony changed hands on his uncoupled fishing rod.

"A bellboy who doubles as a ghillie? It could only happen in Ireland. My rental car is out rear. Let's go!" The American's broad shoulders shook with mirth as he led the way to the car park. Tony's jaw dropped at the array of equipment piled in the back seat of the Ford Mondeo.

"Mr Shanahan, did you bring all this gear from the States?"

"Sure did. Some guys golf; I fish! I've caught everything from blue-fin tuna off Key West, to steelhead trout in Alaska. What do I call you, kid?"

"Tony."

"Hi, Tony, I'm Bill." Tony accepted the proffered hand. Bill's enveloping grip was firm but not severe. "So, Tony, I guess I'm gonna need a permit or something. How do I get fixed up?"

The proprietor of the tackle shop was a shrewd businessman and knew a good thing when he saw one. In ten seconds flat, he had established that, extensive though it was, his customer's knowledge of fish had been gained totally on the other side of the Atlantic. For a good half-hour, Bill got the undivided attention of his keen dark eyes as, one-by-one, each exquisitely tied fly was unhooked from the hat and thoroughly examined, only for the shopkeeper's neatly groomed head to shake in tolerant sympathy.

"Oh, they're lovely flies, sir, beautifully tied... a work of art... Did you tie them yourself? Amazing! You're a gifted man, to be sure... but... you know how it is... horses for courses... different strokes... The problem with fish is this: a fish will only go for what he's accustomed to. These flies represent the types of insects and larvae that you have in America. We wouldn't have nearly as many... Young Tony there could tell you. No, sir, we've nothing like them here at all!"

Bill swallowed it hook, line and sinker and, so engrossed had he become in his buying frenzy that, without Tony's gentle reminder he would have left the premises without the very licence that had brought him there in the first place. Once back in the vehicle, Bill shot a questioning glance at his guide.

"So, not only did you lose your snakes but you're fresh out of bugs too?" The heat rising on Tony's cheeks had little to do with the brilliant sunshine that blazed through the car windows.

"We have some bugs, but not as many as you'd have in America..."

"That's a good answer, kid. I guess all the clever ones didn't emigrate after all. So come on, Tony, you're the guide. Find me some fish!"

"Do you want to fly-fish or spin?"

"Why don't we try a little spinning first, just to get the arms going?" The car swayed as Bill rotated his huge shoulders in anticipation.

"There's a place about two miles back, on the other side of town, we could give it a go there."

"Your call, Tony." After some initial difficulty with the Mondeo's alien gearshift, Bill completed a passable three-point-turn.

Tony proved himself a competent navigator and soon the car was bouncing along the final few yards of the rough stone passage that led to the riverbank. Before Bill made any attempt to set his tackle, he opened the car-boot to reveal a veritable treasure trove of outdoor-wear that would have left the tackle-

3

shop-man speechless. Bill had a question as he donned a beige *great-white-hunter* jacket.

"Does this spot have a name?" He indicated the stretch of mirror-still water before them.

"It's known as *The Otters' Hole*."

"The Otters' Hole." Bill savoured the name. "I thought it would be bigger."

"There are some wider pools nearer town but they wouldn't be as deep. We can go someplace else if you like." Tony got the distinct impression that his words had gone unheard. Bill's eyes seemed to be focussed on some point high up in the distant mountains.

"The Otters' Hole." Bill repeated. "No... no, right here looks good to me." He eased his buttocks against the shimmering rear wing of the vehicle and forced his feet into a pair of green waders. "Ok, kid, you're doing good so far. Why don't you bait up for me and we'll go for it?" The request took Tony off-guard. Bill grinned at the look of confusion on the youth's face. "Come on kid, you're supposed to be the ghillie. It's your turf, your bugs, your call!"

"But what...? I mean... would you prefer a minnow or a flying condom or a German sprat or what?"

"What have you got?" The big man lurched upright, stamping his heels into position inside the waders.

"A blue-and-silver minnow."

"That sounds good to me."

They fished the pool, up and down, for well over an hour without as much as a nibble. Tony cast wearily upstream and winced as a dull pain throbbed beneath the point of his right shoulder. With a sigh, he secured the treble-hook on his first runner and placed the rod against the bumper of the car. Suddenly Bill's voice boomed from his position on the opposite bank.

"Hey, kid, you're not giving up already?"

"It's a total waste of time; there's nothing there."

"Look around you, kid! Don't you see all this beauty right here on your doorstep? Can't you hear the bees, the birdsong?

Can't you smell the flowers, the hay? Would you really prefer to be back in that stuffy hotel right now?"

"No, but..."

"No buts, kid. Life's too short for buts. Take a break and we'll have lunch in thirty minutes!" The whiz and plop of Bill's lure signalled the end of the brief exchange. Tony stretched out on a grassy mound, beneath the shade of a mature willow, and heard and saw and smelled. Soon the daily routine of the hotel seemed light years away...

Tony had no idea how long he had slept but he awoke with a start to find Bill's towering bulk grinning down at him.

"Sorry, Mr. Shanahan, I..."

"A sure sign of a clear conscience, kid... and my friends call me Bill!" Encouraged by Bill's light heartedness, Tony pushed himself up on his elbows.

"Any luck?"

"Not a tiddler but at least we're out in the air." Humming softly, he turned back towards the car. Tony allowed his head to drop back onto the grass for a few minutes before Bill's urgent bellow sent him clambering to his feet. "I didn't bring you out here just to lay about all day!" Mustering apologies, Tony rushed towards the car only for the words to melt in his throat at the scene before him. Bill had laid a tartan rug on the grass and on it he was placing a huge plate of assorted sandwiches. Agape, Tony accepted a steaming mug from the grinning giant before finally recovering his speech.

"What...? How...?"

"The breakfast waitress put it together when I told her that the bellboy was taking me fishing. A gullible Yank might call it a touch of the *céad míle fáiltes* but it's my bet that she's sweet on you!" Bill winked exaggeratedly as he filled his mug from a litre-size thermos flask. "The tea was her idea too; I'd prefer coffee." Tony indicated his mouth, hurriedly stuffed with a ham sandwich, as his excuse not to reply. He need not have worried: it seemed that Bill knew when enough had been said.

Silence reigned until Bill had rinsed the mugs in the river and scattered the surviving morsels of food for the attendant birds to squabble over. As he lit a thick cigar, he shot a sidelong glance in Tony's direction.

"So, Tony. Have you graduated high-school yet?" Each syllable was clouded with little plumes of smoke. Tony breathed deeply, visibly relieved at the change of subject.

"I'll be doing the Leaving Cert next year, in June."

"Then what? Do you have any career plans?"

"A lot will depend on how my results go."

"You'll do good, kid, but I guess there's more than one kind of success. Take today, not a fish in sight but I'm sure having fun."

"Don't give up yet, there's still a lot of river left."

"I'm all set, lead the way!"

Tony decided on a spot about a half-mile upstream. As they neared their destination, Bill became strangely agitated. His eyes darted from side to side of the road and his breath came in short shallow gasps. Without warning, he stamped the car to a skidding halt beside the pillared entrance to a large period house.

"What's...?" Tony's concerned gasp was stifled by the restraining jolt of his seatbelt.

"Are you ok, kid?"

"I'm fine, it's just... Are you all right?" Bill's breathing was still laboured but, when he turned to face his passenger, it was excitement rather than panic that brightened his eyes.

"I'm good, kid. I can't remember when I last felt this good. Could we stop here?

"This is where we're going. There's a passage beyond the house."

"Won't they mind... the folks in the big house?"

"No, these are club waters. We're perfectly legal." This time Bill chose his own spinner and whistled softly as his eyes drank in the hypnotic stretch of tree-lined water. Tony too had noticed the trees but this time he wasn't just looking at birds; his eyes were now straining to identify the different species. Names like: goldfinch, sparrow, blue tit and wagtail formed on his tongue. Swallows and swifts soared and swooped in quest of the clouds

of insects that hovered over the little mud pools at the side of
the shrunken stream.

It was almost two hours before Bill made his way back towards the car. Tony noticed the heaviness of the shortened stride
but the old eyes held a boyish glint.

"I got a bite, just below *The Soldier's Pool*, a good tug but I
just didn't..."

"The Soldier's Pool? I thought you'd never... How...?"

"How do I know that it's called The Soldier's Pool? I recog-
nised the The Otters' Hole too, I just wanted to hear you say
the name. I know this river as well as I know the veins on the
backs of my own hands." Bill laid his rod against an ash sapling
and eased his bulk onto the grass. "The story goes that, in old
Johnson's time, a couple of soldiers from the barracks in town
made a night-raid on the salmon in the pool. Old Johnson spotted them from the big house and crept down with a shotgun.
They say that he fired in the air and the lads panicked. The poor
guys tried to cross at *The Bull's Ford* but one of them must have
missed his step in the darkness. They recovered the body next
morning."

"I've never heard that story. How...?"

"My mother was from here. She emigrated to Liverpool when
she was fifteen and then, a few years later, on to New York.
There she married my father, a Connemara man. He was a cop
but was shot in the line of duty just before I was born. Even as
a baby in the womb, I was big, too big for my mother to birth.
She survived, but only just and she couldn't have any more children after me. The two of us were really close and, night after
night, she'd tell me stories about her home and the landmarks
of her childhood." Bill paused for a moment to catch his breath;
Tony's curiosity was aroused.

"What was her name?

"Mary O'Connor! Her father was Bill, he was the cowman
up at Johnson's."

"My grandmother was O'Connor, we could be..."

"We could maybe do the family tree bit over dinner?"

"I might have cousins in America? Your family...?" Bill's great head shook slowly, his chin drooping lower with each half-turn.

"Sorry, kid, there's only me! Mother died when I was about your age and from then, until six months ago, I was too busy getting rich to think about marriage or children. When I was diagnosed, I decided to sell the lot and come over here for Mother's fiftieth anniversary; it's today!"

"Diagnosed?" The question was out before Tony could stop himself.

"Yes, kid, the *Big C*! They said that, with Chemo, I might get a year. Well, I've managed six months without it, so I guess every moment from here on is a bonus. So come on, kid. My guess is that *The Badger's Inch* is about a mile upstream."

Bill assembled his fly rod and, with a quirky grin, added an unlikely looking specimen from his headgear to the pair he and Tony had already selected from the new stock. An instant after the third graceful cast, Tony heard Bill's reel scream as a well-timed strike set the barb of the American fly in the gaping jaw of the elusive quarry. The superbly game creature leapt high into the air before making a dash towards the cover of a little clump of bulrushes beside the far bank. Bill allowed the fish run until the tension eased on the line. Slowly, carefully, the experienced angler began to rewind, constantly alert for the fish's next surge for freedom. For twenty minutes, Tony marvelled at the struggle between instinct and craft until the resistance of the salmon was eventually broken by the lethal combination of man and technology. Silently, Tony held the landing net in readiness until Bill deemed the moment right to finally land his prize. Even as he grabbed the net, Bill was thinking a move ahead.

"Tony, bring that camera from the glove-box!" In the seconds that Tony was absent, Bill had not only landed the salmon but had crouched to a classic angler's pose with the fish held on display across his chest. "Hurry, Tony, get a few shots... good boy... good... just one more... Yes!" Tony watched incredulously as the American splashed back into the shallows, leaned forward and gently lowered the exhausted creature to the water.

Bill manoeuvred the salmon in the current for a few moments then straightened painfully, wiping his hands on his jacket.

"You let him go?" Tony winced at the disapproval in his own voice. Bill took a few shambling steps forward, before flopping wearily to his knees.

"Tony, of the three of us: you me and that fish, which two have most in common?" The wheezed words were barely audible.

"I suppose, you and I, we're..."

"Human? Yes, but that's a young salmon, a grilse, making his first trip back to fresh water since he went to sea as a smolt, perhaps five years ago. I guess, you could say that he's just graduated high school. What right would I have to cut him off, after he has battled to survive the dangers of thousands of miles, trying to get home to the very spawning grounds where he was hatched? Mark my words, Tony, when you set out on the voyage of life, there will be fat old codgers waiting for you too, waiting to lure you into their net, with all the newest gadgets from the tackle shop. I took their baits, I took their dollars and I took their crap, while they took my time... my lifetime. Now, it's too late for..." Bill lurched violently forward, his bowed frame jerking with each racking cough. After few laboured breaths, he continued – red faced – in a hoarse whisper. "They'll want your time too, Tony, and you'll be tempted but, wherever life takes you, just remember this: no amount of salty sea can ever compensate for a single mouthful of fresh water!"

INNOCENT SIN

A new home, they said; *in September*, they said, but what were they talking about? Besides, September was only seven weeks away. It was a place where she could attend school and receive the best of medical care, all under the same roof, they said. But Jane didn't want a new home, she was fairly happy with the one she already had. Well... it had been even better before the baby...

It was now five years since the birth of her brother had shattered the equilibrium of Jane's life, just before her seventh birthday. The sanctuary of sleep had been the first victim: night after exhausting night, the infant's wailing would trigger bouts of hushed, animated bickering followed by the slamming of doors, the pounding of stairs and the frenzied rattling of kitchen utensils, before an all-too-brief interlude of surreal calm. The sounds that followed were even more unnerving: tiptoeing feet, creaking floorboards and squeaking hinges, all of which emphasised the isolation of Jane's box bedroom from the rest of the household.

From the very outset, Trevor's presence had brought an abrupt end to Jane's favourite pursuit of watching cartoons with the TV turned up really loud. Gradually her bedtime stories became less frequent, and her lovely evening walks with Dad, along by the lake, soon became a vague memory. Nowadays, it seemed that Trevor was central to everything that happened in the world.

He was the perfect child, one that any parent could be proud of, could take anywhere, to meet anyone. Trevor could run, he could kick a football, he could do little jobs for Mum about the house... Nobody ever spoke about finding a residential home for Trevor; everybody loved Trevor, and soon they would be able to love him even more.

She watched her brother now from her position at the end of the wooden jetty. Mum would be angry if she knew the children's precise whereabouts, this part of the lake was strictly out-of-bounds. Everybody knew it was here that the dark waters swirled to their greatest depths. Jane sighed in frustration; it was all so unfair. There was Trevor, gleefully hurling stone after stone at the piece of driftwood that bobbed on the lake surface, while she was forced to sit and watch from her prison on wheels. If only she still had Scruffy for company, life would be almost bearable. How she had loved that little dog... and how he had adored her in return. Scruffy's love had been unconditional: when those soft dark eyes looked up at her they saw only the person, never the condition. Whenever she would throw a ball or a stick, the shaggy little mongrel would scamper off to retrieve it and then stand up on his hind legs to deliver the prize into her good left hand.

Scruffy had loved everyone, even two-year-old Trevor. Despite the fact that the toddler was prone to bouts of ear and tail pulling, Scruffy never retaliated. The dog's response to such treatment was to seek sanctuary behind an armchair or sofa until his tormentor had found some new distraction. It was about this time that Trevor had fallen ill. Jane had to admit that she had derived a strange satisfaction from watching her brother splutter and gasp when his asthma attacks were at their worst. She had philosophically endured the extra demands which these seizures made on her parents... in anticipation of the unscheduled treats that came her way: ice-cold lollies, tubes of chewy wine gums and crackling bags of potato crisps. *Just to keep her quiet*, they would say before hurrying back to minister to the more pressing needs of their favourite.

It was the doctor who had made the earth-shattering announcement. Trevor was allergic to the dog. Not a single word about Dad's pipe or Mum's cigarettes, oh no... it was all Scruffy's fault. All three adults were adamant that the dog would have to go. But where was he to go?

We'll find him a new home! Dad had muttered hopefully.

Out in the country! Mum had added with finality. That night, Jane hugged Scruffy for the final time before crying herself to sleep to the sound of Trevor's wheezing from Mum's room, across the hallway.

Next morning, Jane was left in bed a little longer than usual. She heard Dad's car drive off but was puzzled when it returned to the driveway about a half-an-hour later. She strained her ears in a vain effort to overhear her parents' heated exchanges from the kitchen but failed to detect any reference to *the country*, although *the vet* was mentioned more than once.

He's much happier now; dogs prefer the country! Mum had assured her at breakfast but, while Mum appeared genuinely pleased at Scruffy's good fortune, Dad was less enthusiastic and had avoided his daughter's gaze for several days afterwards.

After Scruffy's departure, every excursion to the country brought renewed hope that the little dog's whereabouts might be confirmed. On each eagerly anticipated occasion, Jane analysed every distant bark or fleeting glimpse of a wagging tail with disappointing results. In truth, she had suspected the worst from the beginning and had almost resigned herself to the harsh reality that Scruffy was no more. She had seen on TV that vets sometimes do more than make sick animals better... but one should never abandon hope... without hope, there was nothing...

It was the peace that rocked Jane back to the present; Trevor had suddenly become unbelievably quiet. The summer afternoon was now embellished with the rival tones of numerous unseen songbirds, a world away from the boy's irritating impressions of fighter planes and exploding missiles. It took some time for Jane's eyes to locate her brother's position. He had moved back from the lakeshore and now his combat jacket was barely distinguishable from the dense undergrowth at the edge of the copse that separated the lake from the busy main road that led to the rest of the universe. Without warning, Trevor began to jump and shout... something about spiders and ants. Clearly not expecting a response from his sister, he dropped back down on all fours and resumed his explorations among the thickets.

A sudden commotion on the water below grabbed Jane's attention. A startled moorhen seemed to tread the lake surface before scuttling, squawking in protest, towards the opposite shore. The cause of the creature's panic was soon evident: a cob mute swan paddled from beneath the jetty with wings raised and neck stretched aggressively forward. The territorial bird was quickly followed by his mate and their brood of six grey downy cygnets. Instantly, Jane regretted not having as much as a crust of bread to offer the swan family. Jane loved all birds but especially swans. These graceful creatures had been her favourites ever since Dad had first read *The Ugly Duckling* story to her, in happier times. How she had wished that one morning she too would marvel at the type of reflected miracle that had transformed the ugly duckling into a beautiful swan. So often she had dreamt of waking up to find a pair of sturdy legs, a right hand that would respond to her brain and a mouth that could smile, or at least change expression from the perpetual leer she had grown to hate.

Prior to Trevor's birth, she hadn't really been aware of her shortcomings. Back then, her parents' lives had seemed to revolve around hers and sometimes Dad would call her *little princess*... especially after reading the story of *Cinderella*. Jane had often wondered what it would be like to have a sister... or even an ugly stepsister; surely anything would have been an improvement on Trevor. But those days were long gone, and with them had gone her belief in the wonderful powers of magic wands and fairy godmothers. Instead of a promise, the future was increasingly becoming a threat.

Blinking to clear her vision, she watched the swans glide silently towards the shore, the proud male showing the way while the pen kept a watchful brief from the rear of the little parade. Trevor's re-emergence from his sojourn in his personal jungle was an unhappy coincidence. With a whoop of delight, he manned his coastal battlements and proceeded to launch a merciless barrage against the would-be invaders of his kingdom. Sticks, stones, plastic bottles and virtually anything else that wasn't restrained by roots, bolts or nails was commandeered and deployed as ammunition against the unfortunate swan family. The birds, accustomed as they were to having bread and other treats thrown to them by more friendly humans, increased their speed towards the shore as Trevor's missiles continued to fall well short of the intended victims. Horrified, Jane gaped as the gap between safety and danger continued to dwindle... She wanted to call out... to warn the swans... to threaten her brother... to... to do something... anything... but no words would come...

Then the odds suddenly took a vital swing in the swans' favour. It appeared that Trevor had simply run out of ammunition before the enemy had come within range of his fusillade. Abandoning his fortress, he made a strategic retreat to the cover of the canopy to replenish his armoury for one final assault against the flotilla that steamed relentlessly towards his shore. Though hidden from her view by the abundant foliage, Jane could still monitor Trevor's progress by the telltale death-throes of each doomed sapling that fell to his eager hands. Moments later, Jane began to breath more easily. Not only had the swans altered their course back towards the safety of the centre of the lake but there was also a marked lack of activity from Trevor's direction.

Welcome though the lull was, it proved all too brief. Trevor's leafy glade seemed to erupt with an ear-shattering scream. Was he experimenting with some new kind of war cry? Trevor burst from the greenery, his arms flailing wildly about his head, and hit the jetty running hard. Nobody knew the extent of Trevor's repertoire of personae better than Jane, but his present antics had her stumped. Onwards he charged, wailing shamelessly, his curved fingers clawing as if at some great invisible cobweb. Then she heard it, despite Trevor's cries and the hollow thudding of his runners on the seasoned boards of the jetty, it was unmistakable: the buzzing of enraged wasps... a *lot* of enraged wasps... and he was leading them directly towards *her*! She simply had to do something and she had to do it now.

Frantically, her good left hand flew to the basket that hung from the handles of her wheelchair; feverishly, her fingers groped deep within the unseen depths somewhere behind the small of her back. She could see individual wasps now, as plain as the terror in the boy's eyes. Even as her fingers tightened around their target, she tugged her hand free of the basket and swung it forward as she had done so many times when throwing a ball for Scruffy.

Jane had a brief glimpse of Trevor's *Action Man* soaring towards its owner's head. Trevor's reactions were a fraction too slow; *Action Man* took him full on the right cheek, causing him to lurch sideways against the decaying guardrail of the jetty. As the fragile wood shattered, the camouflaged figures of boy and toy seemed to swim in thin air before hitting the water with a resounding splash. Jane sat stock still while a couple of wasps whizzed about her ears before finally veering back towards their nest.

Engaging her motor, Jane manoeuvred her chair forward until she could clearly see Trevor's life's breath bubble to the surface. It took some time for the water to grow still but she waited a few more minutes before selecting her mother's number on her mobile phone...

MAIDEN HURDLES

"Will you sing one?" While the girl's dark eyes mirrored Declan's smile, her answer was the same as when he had first asked the question, five years before.

"I've nothing to sing about!"

"Hah! Anyway, it's great to see you, Áine. How are the other two, are they here?"

"Oh yes, we three…"

"All for one… Some things never change!"

"Unfortunately!" Her eyes rolled. "They're putting on the glad-rags. Will we see you at the hotel later, or are you still in love?"

"Maybe and… yes!"

"Well, just in case, you'd better sing my song now." She indicated her wristwatch. "I must head."

"I hope the town is ready for another week of *The ABC girls.*" He swung back to the microphone and delivered his rendition of *Black is the Colour.* She joined in the chorus and led the applause before smiling her thanks as she melted through the crowd.

Two hours later, he shouldered his way through the phalanx of owners, trainers, punters, hawkers and chancers that poured from the closing Ballybunion hostelries. The variety of accents that echoed through the streets was proof that this was no ordinary gathering; this was Listowel Race Week, the final festival meeting of the year, the farmers' annual holiday.

He glowed inwardly at the prospect of meeting the girls again: Bernie, the striking, demure, blonde nurse, Claire, the voluptuous, red-haired civil servant and Áine, the banker of the sloe-black eyes and ready smile. He frowned at the heaving throng that milled around the hotel's main entrance. Slipping around the side of the building, he thumbed the keypad of his mobile phone. A moment later a broadening stream of light betrayed the clandestine opening of the kitchen service door. Whispering his thanks, he tucked a tenner into the breast pocket of the night porter's shirt and stepped inside.

A shout from Áine saved him from the chaotic scrum at the bar counter. Enticingly, she flourished a pint of lager from her corner table.

"You were very sure that I'd turn up." He said, embracing each girl in turn.

"Well, I thought you looked... thirsty." Áine slid a stool from its hiding place beneath the table.

"Thanks for the drink. It's great to see you all again; more beautiful than ever." A little splash of colour brightened Bernie's cheeks.

"Still the old charmer, Declan." Claire purred seductively.

"Like the guitar, it's part of his act." Áine wrist rose and fell in a strumming motion.

"A least it means that I get to meet gorgeous women like you." He raised his glass in salute before taking a long grateful swallow.

"So, how's the love life these days?" He turned to face the challenge of Claire's enquiring gaze.

"I can't complain. And yourself?" Her arms waved dismissively.

"I'm still hanging around with these two. What does that tell you?"

"What about that Offaly rover you met last year?"

"He went home on the Sunday morning, probably to take his wife and kids to Mass!"

"Oops, sorry!"

"She's welcome to him; he snores!" Bernie scowled.

"And farts!" Áine added, wrinkling her nose at the recollection.

"Áine!" Bernie blushed again; Declan attempted to change the subject.

"So, how's the *craic* in Galway these days?"

"Oh, so-so. You still haven't visited us; not even a bloody phone call!" A thrill surged through his body as Claire's petulant pout belied the recrimination in her words.

"The summer was just too busy. I haven't had a weekend off since before Easter!"

"There were six whole months between October and April!" Áine added her weight to Claire's remark.

"I bet you found time for the *Willie Clancy* thing!" Claire was determined not to let it rest.

"I managed a couple of days, mid-week, but couldn't make the weekend."

"We went to Tubbercurry but all we saw was a bunch of women playing *diddle-dee-i* music." Bernie's digression inadvertently provided him with an opportunity to evade the inquisition.

"Ah, that's the *trad* scene for you. Tell me, did any of you back that winner I gave you for *The Slán Abhaile* race last year?"

"No, we don't back horses!" He gasped in disbelief at Bernie's words.

"You go to a race meeting and don't back horses?" He glanced from one shaking head to another.

"We don't actually go racing!" He studied Bernie's wide blue eyes for a hint of a wind-up, there was none.

"You come all the way from Galway, for the craziest week of the year, and you have no interest in racing? What do you do with yourselves all day?" Claire decided it was her turn to answer.

"We have a holiday! We party all night, sleep till lunchtime, then we hit the beach, come back for dinner and party all over again. It's perfect!"

"I don't understand... Why...?"

"Look around you; what do you see?" Áine was revelling in his confusion.

"I see a lot of people!"

"A lot of *male* people, I'd say that the men in this room outnumber the women by about four to one. Those odds I can live with!"

"But if it's men you're after, why don't you take a holiday earlier in the year. Say in July or August?"

"Too much competition!" It was Áine who replied.

"From tourists?"

"From teachers!" Claire's carefully glossed lips curled vengefully as she spat the words.

"Teachers?" His question was Bernie's cue.

"Farmers go for teachers in a big way, it's *the laying hen* syndrome! A steady salary, a short working day, which means they can ferry the kids to and from school, and they have long summer holidays, at a time when they're most needed on the land! They say that marrying a teacher is worth twenty cows to a farmer!" Declan flinched at the unprecedented venom of her tone.

"I'm sure they're taught it in agricultural college!" Claire added. Blonde and dark tresses danced in agreement.

"You can't be serious?"

"What does your girlfriend do?" Áine eyed him levelly.

"She's a teacher but..."

"Well, there you are; you're all at it!" Claire and Bernie nodded their support.

"Her job has nothing to do with it!" His pleading eyes flitted from one accusing face to another. Áine had a further question.

"Did you know she was a teacher before or after your first date?"

"Well, before but..." His admission was met with silent condemnation.

"I'm going for a smoke!" Claire conjured a cigarette from her handbag and concealed it furtively in her half-closed fist.

"I'll go with you." Bernie was already on her feet.

"You don't smoke!" Áine gasped.

"I don't do anything and I'm just about sick of it! Claire, are you coming?" Claire shrugged and, stuffing her cigarette packet into the pocket of her jeans, followed the bristling blonde towards the exit.

"Wow! What was that about?" Declan asked, his eyes still trained on the girls' backs.

"Bernie used to be engaged to a farmer back home. It broke up about five years ago, shortly before our first trip here. I thought she was over it but he got married last month... to a teacher!"

"Oh!"

"Yeah. Anyway, I take it you're not driving home tonight... not after drinking pints?"

"No, I have a bed over the pub."

"Won't your teacher friend mind?"

"We don't actually live together, she works in Limerick."

"How convenient for you. You've got it all figured out; the best of both worlds!"

"It's not perfect but it works."

"Well, that's all right, then. I suppose you've already got somebody lined up for later?"

"What?"

"Don't play the innocent with me. I saw you chatting up that blonde last year!"

"I talk to a lot of women; it goes with the territory!"

"The fringe benefits of the wandering minstrel!"

"I wish!"

"So, what about it?" Provocation gleamed in Áine's eyes.

"What about what?" He finally managed.

"It looks like we're both free, so how about you and me... tonight! Don't try to deny that you fancy me a bit; I've known it since that very first night at your gig! Were you in a relationship then?"

"No, I don't think so... well maybe. What does it matter anyway?"

"Earlier, back in the pub, when I asked you if you were still in love, you said *maybe*!"

"No, I said that *maybe* I'd come to the hotel!"

"Humph! So why did you come to the hotel?"

"I fancied a late pint and a chat with three beautiful women, whom I regard as friends."

"Yeah, right! You fancy Claire too, don't you; maybe even Bernie? Which one of us do you fancy the most?"

"This is crazy!"

"If Claire made you an offer, what would you do?"

"Ah, Áine!"

"What if it was Claire... *and* me... *together*?"

"Wha...?"

"That got your attention but don't get too excited. It's not an option!"

"Do you make a habit of seducing other women's boyfriends?"

"Especially teachers' boyfriends! Look, Declan, I've got no desire to rock your cosy little boat; I'd just like to get laid tonight and, if you're up for it, it would save us both a lot of time!"

"Ah, a sneaky one-night-stand and back to normal tomorrow?"

"Well, if we were good together... and ... ah shit! Now, I want a cigarette!" She finished her lager in a gulp. "Just think about it!" She stifled a burp and sped towards the exit.

"Wow!" He muttered and braced himself to face the crush at the counter.

Claire and Bernie made their reappearance as Declan returned with the tray of drinks.

"What did you get up to with Áine?" His innocent shrug cut no ice with Claire. "Well, whatever you said to her, she's pumping!"

"Claire, don't!" Bernie pleaded.

"Relax, Bernie, we're all adults here!" The springy red curls swung back towards Declan. "She propositioned you, didn't she?"

"Claire!" Bernie's face was a deep crimson.

"Look, it's all right! She was going to do make a move on you last year, before she got lucky with that bookie from Kildare!"

"I don't believe this!" Declan gestured helplessly.

"And you're supposed to be a man of the world?"

"I'm going to the ladies!" Bernie sprang to her feet and battled her way through the sea of bodies. Claire was unrelenting.

"There's definitely something stirring between the pair of you, there's no point in trying to deny it. Áine never smokes except when there is sex in the air; spill it!"

"What are you like?" He took a nervous swallow from his glass.

"Would it surprise you to hear that she's afraid that you and I might have a thing?"

"Nothing would surprise me at this stage!"

"That's confirmation enough for me. So, are you up for it?"

"For what?"

"You and Áine... unless you've got something else..."

"Christ, you're a bunch of raving nymphomaniacs!"

"The bloody hypocrisy of it! Men proposition women all the time and nobody bats an eyelid. Whatever happened to equality of the sexes?"

"Is this mine?" Neither was aware of Áine's return until she placed a balancing hand on Declan's shoulder and leaned across to take her fresh drink from the table. "I've gotta go, I'm sure you'll manage fine without me. Declan, will I see you tomorrow?"

"Tomorrow? I suppose..." If she heard, she gave no indication. Declan wondered at his brief pang of jealousy as his eyes followed Áine to where a tall, fair-haired man guarded an armchair in readiness for her arrival.

"Hard luck, *Decko*," Claire punched him playfully on the shoulder. "I think you've just been pipped at the post! Hey, what's so funny?" Declan was indeed chuckling but whether it was with relief at this sudden twist of fate or something more intriguingly complex, he was not quite sure.

"You won't believe this; I can hardly believe it myself!"

"What?" Claire prompted.

"That guy with Áine, I know him and guess what?"

"What?"

"He's a *teacher*!"

"I know..." her lip curled again, "and so is his *wife*!"

Good Intentions

"My God, what's the world coming to?" Joan lent her customary deaf ear to Darby's reactions to the latest news scandals. Drying the second dinner plate, she hummed along softly with the signature tune of her favourite TV soap. This was the best part of her day: those few hours of companionable silence in front of the television, broken only by Darby's occasional mutterings from behind his tabloid newspaper, or her own intermittent words of matronly advice to some character in a screen drama. Between her selected programmes, there was time for reflection.

Both sets of parents had been against their early marriage.

'You're barely out of your teens!' her father had said.

'I can't see why, if she's not even pregnant!' was Darby's mother's mantra. Yet, here they were, over thirty years later, alone in the world again since Shane, their youngest, had followed the footsteps of his brother and sister to the college in the city.

Yes, she thought, sneaking a satisfied glance at her husband's picture of domestic bliss, *we didn't do too badly after all.*

As the credits rolled, she lowered the volume and turned to Darby.

"Are you going for a pint tonight?" He placed his folded newspaper on the coffee table and checked his wristwatch against the pendulum clock above the mantelpiece.

"Ah, I don't think I'll bother." He stretched his arms and leaned his shoulders back against his armchair.

"But it's Friday... and a long weekend..."

"I know, but... You go on ahead, love, I might take a stroll later."

"No, I wasn't looking for an escort; I'm meeting the girls tonight. I just thought you might like a pint, you haven't been out for weeks."

23

"Woman, will you listen to yourself? Most men of my age have wives who nag them to exercise more and drink less, not the other way around!"

"I wasn't saying that at all... Of course, I'm delighted you're looking after yourself... you're as fit as you've ever been, but I do wish you'd wear your new jacket instead of Díarmuid's old rag."

"Ah sure, who'd be looking at me anyway?" Removing his reading glasses, he pushed himself upright and stamped the sleep from a stockinged foot. "Will you have a cuppa?"

"No, thanks, love!" She replied from the hallway, returning a moment later with the aforementioned garment in her hand.

"What are you doing with that?"

"Well, if you insist on wearing it, I can at least try to make it look a bit more presentable." She rummaged in the sideboard for her sewing basket.

"I don't know what you're fussing for, 'tis fine out the way it is!" He pressed a spoon against the teabag in his *World's Best Dad* mug.

"Go on with you; it's no bother at all!" Suddenly, she sighed. "Where did I put that red reel? Ah well, I suppose a bit of white will have to do." Resuming her seat, she began to replace the frayed stitching on the fading *Liverpool FC* logo, smiling at her ingenuity when, over a decade earlier, she had first employed the badge to conceal the two-inch tear in the right sleeve of her firstborn's black windcheater.

On the village street, a sudden cold breath heralded November's imminent arrival. Tugging her woollen scarf tighter around her throat, Joan marvelled at the resilience of the little posses of miniature masked monsters who braved the elements in quest of trick-or-treat booty. On reaching the pub, she sighed as the welcoming warmth caressed her cheeks. Her arrival was greeted by a little flurry of waving from the corner table: Ina, tall and elegant, in a white lace blouse and navy slacks; the squat Noelle in a frumpy pink sweater and faded blue denims. Unzipping her waxed jacket to reveal a slate-grey pinafore, Joan made a beeline for the counter to observe their time-honoured custom: when you joined the company, you bought a round.

While waiting for her order to be completed, Joan thrilled at how her deep friendship with the girls continued to flourish despite they being several years her junior. Stealing a glance at herself in the mirror behind a row of spirit bottles, she was reassured by what she saw. Yes, she affirmed, even if her natural brunette had paled to a more manageable blonde, she did not look out of place in the company of the younger women.

After a chorus of *cheers* and *sláintes*, the conversation flowed freely. Dark-eyed Ina had a question.

"I suppose you've got a houseful for the weekend?"

"No, thank you very much!" Joan retorted, "Isn't it enough that I'll have the lot for Christmas? Díarmuid and Jane are spending the weekend with her people, Siobhán is gone off to the sun and Shane has a football match." Noelle's tawny curls bobbed understandingly.

"I know, girl. I wish I could send my gang someplace for a few days... or a week... or longer!" She took a quick swallow from her pint of lager. "Isn't it great how quickly Shane has settled in."

"He was always a great mixer!" Ina added.

"Yes, he is that. He reminds me a lot of Darby when he was that age." Joan savoured a mouthful of red wine. Yes, life was good...

It was about a half-hour later that Joan broached a subject that had been concerning her of late.

"Any sign of Helen recently?"

"Helen?" Noelle spluttered a little spray of froth onto the polished table.

"What would she be doing with boring people like us, now that she's a free woman again?" Ina asked with a sneer.

"Ina!" Joan scolded. "It's not her fault that Jack decided to shack up with that little trollop!"

"Maybe he had his reasons!"

"Ina!" This time it was Noelle who reacted.

"Yes, Ina." Joan seconded. "Come on, the three of you grew up together, we should at least give her the benefit of the doubt!" Ina's eyes rolled skyward.

"The benefit of the doubt? Between *the benefit of the doubt* and *the good word*, you refuse to see a fault in anyone!"

"Look, Ina. Who knows what goes on behind closed doors?" Joan rallied.

"Or *outside* them..." Ina hissed from the rim of her brandy balloon.

"What's that supposed to mean?"

"She doesn't mean anything, Joan. Ignore her!" Noelle said, furtively swinging her right shoe towards Ina's shin.

"Has either of you even lifted the phone to her in the last month?" Joan's accusing eyes darted from one to the other. Ina shrugged dismissively; Noelle took a deep swallow from her glass before clearing her throat with ominous deliberation.

"Look, Joan. As wives, we should all be wary of grass widows!"

"Wary? How do you mean *wary*?" The determined set of Joan's jaw suggested that she wasn't going to quit until she got an answer. Ina saw an escape route and grasped it.

"It's my round. The same again?" Once clear of the table, she took a deep breath, puffed her cheeks and exhaled noisily.

"Well?" As Joan's eyes burned into her, Noelle's gaze fell to study the peeling varnish on her uneven finger nails.

"Women in that position are a magnet for men, especially *married* men!"

"Ah, the curse of the other woman! What about the men, Noelle? Do you mean to tell me that if Darby or Bryan or Ina's Kevin started playing around, it would be some woman's fault and not theirs? I don't think so and, in many cases, it's the wives that are to blame!"

"There you are, that's what I'm trying to say. Whatever about your good intentions, you have to face the possibility that it could have been Helen's fault that Jack strayed in the first place!"

"Ah, Noelle, you're twisting my words!"

"Even the road to hell is paved with good intentions!" Both heads swivelled at the sound of Ina's voice. "She's right, Joan. When something like this happens, there's bound to be a chain reaction... and you can imagine the repercussions it could have in a little community of this size!"

"You're both over-reacting. I'm surprised at you. I've only known Helen for a few years but you went to school with her. You can't just abandon a lifelong friend like that. I'm going to phone her right now!" Joan fished her mobile from her handbag and thumbed the keypad. The others remained silent until Joan had disconnected.

"Well?" Ina prompted.

"Her mobile is powered off. What's her landline number again?"

"I'll do it!" Noelle offered, activating her own phone. "It's ringing... ringing... yes! No, it's the bloody machine. She must be out on the razz!" Ina seized the opportunity to change the subject.

"Hey, there's a late disco over in Crowley's! Seeing as how the boys are babysitting, we should make a night of it!"

"I'm game!" Noelle drained her glass in one prodigious gulp.

"No, you two go on ahead. I'm tired, I think I'll just head home." It was only a white lie but how could she tell them that they had knocked all the good out of her evening?

Still fuming at the girls' condemnation of their friend, Joan poured her remaining wine back into its bottle and started homewards. What had come over the girls anyway? If everyone took their attitude, what could be said about two young married women spending the night disco dancing without their husbands? Darby would understand; Darby always understood. But for the grace of God, any one of them could be in Helen's predicament. Even as she closed her hall door, she knew she would have to wait a little longer for Darby's reassurance. A loud snore from upstairs was clear indication that her husband was already asleep. Sighing, she retrieved the little wine bottle from her bag and pensively poured a solitary nightcap.

27

After much agonising, Joan finally reached her decision as the eggs whitened in the pan. There was no need to bother Darby with the girls' behaviour. No, this call was hers alone, she didn't need anybody else's approval; she knew she was right and knowing was enough. Her mind suddenly at ease, she brought Darby his Saturday treat of breakfast in bed and, after breezing through her remaining chores, headed for the shops.

About an hour later, Joan rang Helen's doorbell and waited. A *PlayStation* revved through the open sitting room window and an orange-crayoned, paper pumpkin fluttered inside the frosted-glass of the door. At her second ring, muffled footsteps danced down the stairs.

"Joan!" Helen coughed a lungful of smoke, adjusting the belt of her revealing dressing gown.

"Oh, I'm sorry, Helen! Did I wake you?" Helen drew deeply on her cigarette before flicking it past her visitor to the little patch of unkempt grass at the side of the doorstep.

"Oh no, I was just ... upstairs. I thought it was the milkman calling for his money." She indicated the purse in her left hand.

"I won't come in, I can see you're busy. I was just wondering if you'd like to come out for a drink tonight." Helen slipped the purse into the pocket of a red leather jacket that hung from the banister pillar.

"I'm afraid I can't, my sister is coming for the weekend... But thanks anyway!" Helen managed a tight smile, pointedly taking a backward step.

"That will be nice for you. Well, enjoy the weekend!" As Joan began to turn, Helen brushed against the red jacket; almost in slow motion, it began to slip, then gathered speed. Helen's reaction was a milli-second too slow. As the jacket flopped to the floor, both women stared in horror at the *Liverpool FC* logo, secured to the right sleeve of the black windcheater, with even white stitches...

ILL WINDS

I had heard many terms used to describe harsh winds but none could even approach doing justice to the bone-chilling blasts that now tore at my shins. Gritting my teeth, I forced my body sideways from the partial protection of my open car door and took a few hesitant steps towards my ancestral home. As a distant descendant of a disgraced third son, the chances of my ever even seeing *Ravenswood House* had been, at best, remote but now it seemed that fate had decreed that the imposing mansion before me was to be my unlikely inheritance.

My presence had not gone unnoticed. Even as my polished city shoes disappeared into the sinkhole that had once been an entrance avenue, the budding branches above my head erupted in a cacophony of alarm calls. The scene could have been snipped from a reel of Hitchcock's *The Birds*. The be-ruffled, black-plumed bodies were everywhere... squabbling, squawking, cackling, cawing... For a fanciful moment I entertained the illusion that I was gazing at the very ravens for which the estate had been originally named.

Then the hailstones came; like so many icy shotgun pellets, they stung my ears, my nose, my forehead and my cheeks, propelled by the razor gusts of relentless squalls. That was it, I had seen enough for one day. Eager to flee the eerie scene, I dragged my numbed feet through the clinging mire, back to the car. As I reversed towards the perceived safety of the main road, I could have sworn that a grimy curtain twitched in a second floor window.

"Mr. Hillman, welcome!" The elderly solicitor's grip belied his frail frame. "It's a pleasure to finally meet the new master of Ravenswood. When would you like to view the property?" He motioned me towards a leather armchair.

"Thanks... but no, I've just had a look... I don't think it's quite my scene. Tell me, what's the approximate value of the place?"

"Oh, well... the house, cottages, outbuildings and lands? I suppose, even in today's climate, you could be looking at somewhere in the region of four million euro... three million sterling!" It was much more than I had dared hope.

"How soon can you put it on the market?"

"On the market? Oh no, you can't sell."

"But I thought the property was freehold."

"It is, but the title deeds have been... am... mislaid or lost!"

"Mislaid, lost? Did they ever exist?"

"My grandfather's old records show that we once held them for safe keeping but Sir Robert removed them shortly after the foundation of the Free State; he had concerns about how a nationalist government might view the old ascendancy. Charlie spent a lifetime searching for them... but no good!"

No good! The words exploded like cannon fire in my brain, blasting to oblivion my dreams of a Fulham town house, a vintage Aston Martin and my escape route from my soulless position in a colourless London bank.

"But there's a good living to be had. " The solicitor strove manfully to dilute my disappointment. "Charlie left the place in good shape. Ravenswood has the best farmland in this part of the county... you'll have people queuing up to rent it... and you could convert the house into a hotel... or maybe even develop a golf club. The yard would suit a horse trainer; sure, old Charlie was well into his seventies when he trained that chestnut mare to win *over-the-banks* at Punchestown!"

I had originally planned to spend a few days in the area, just long enough to see a *For Sale* sign erected at Ravenswood House. Now, even that plan was shattered. I needed time... to think... to digest the news.

The hotel manager was genuinely sympathetic but equally adamant: he was fully booked from Friday through Sunday – for some fishing thing. I could have my room for one more night but then... Deciding to review old Charlie's legacy in the light of my new circumstances, I thought it wise to be properly attired for my return to Ravenswood.

The store proprietor beamed at my selections: weatherproof jacket and hat and a pair of sturdy wellington boots.

"You'll land a big one for sure!" he cooed, returning my stressed credit card. I nodded, thinking, *I already have, but what am I going to do with it?*

The illusion of grandeur faded with each squelching step along the overgrown avenue. The aura of degeneration was almost tangible: window frames, facia boards and the exquisitely crafted front porch, all showed signs of irreversible decay. From a railed paddock, an in-foal chestnut mare whinnied a welcome, almost in tune with the whine of the wind. I rapped on the peeling paint of the door, there was no response; after a short pause, I tried again, this time with more vigour, but the result was the same. It was then that I noticed what looked like an old bucket handle, dangling from a few links of rusted chain. On impulse, I yanked on the apparatus and was rewarded with a distant chime, which sounded remarkably like the bell of my late grandaunt's bicycle. Somewhere within, a dog gave a couple of hoarse barks and, almost instantaneously, a disembodied female voice rang out.

"*Around the back!*" I obeyed and found myself entering a different world. A neat cobbled yard stretched from the rear of the house to a sizeable stable block and outbuildings. A glossy black cat uncurled to eye me balefully from the bonnet of a red Ford Fiesta, parked possessively close to the rear entrance to the house. The freshly painted maroon door opened at my approach and, for a few spine-chilling seconds, I thought I was looking at the reincarnation of my old granddad's big sister...

"Yes?" The spectral apparition demanded. She stood ramrod-straight, her silver hair drawn severely back into a tight bun, accentuating her strong angular features.

Of course, I thought, *you would have a black cat!*

"Well?" She prompted, her steel-grey eyes searing through me.

"Good day," I managed, "I'm Rob Hillman."

"You'd better come in." With a final glare at my muddied boots, she shrugged and spun back indoors, her grey housecoat swishing with every step. Removing my offending footwear, I forced my stockinged feet across the cold terracotta tiles.

"I suppose you could be a Hillman." She finally conceded. An ancient liver-and-white spaniel yawned what could have been a breathless agreement from his wicker basket beside a radiating AGA cooker. She waved me towards a plain wooden chair.

"Oh, I am! I have documentation."

"And you sound like one!" She selected a large log from the pile beside the cooker, her hand rising and falling as if to gauge its weight.

"That's a great stove;" I ventured, fearing for my safety. "Isn't that wind something else?" My shiver was genuine.

"It's a lazy wind!" She said, lifting the ring of the AGA.

"Lazy?" I gasped, feeling a little braver now that the log seemed destined for the cooker. "It seemed pretty lively to me!"

"It's a lazy wind!" She jammed the chunk of ash into the firebox, raising a shower of sparks. "Too lazy to go around you, so it just cuts straight through!"

"That's a fair description." I agreed, but she hadn't quite finished with me.

"I'll tell you about documentation, Mr. Hillman. That old dog there has a pedigree that stretches back to Methuselah, so have those horses abroad in the fields. Let me tell you, Mr. Hillman, I'd pay a sight more heed to what their papers say than I would to any human family tree!"

"But..."

"Young man, I know nothing of you or where you've come from, but I do know about the Hillmans. There isn't an idiot on this side of the mountain who doesn't know that my mother was sired by Black Bob, *Sir Robert* to you... no, don't look shocked, 'twas nearly compulsory for his ilk to impregnate the servant girls... and it led to many a local lad being hastily and happily wed! But it wasn't all one-way traffic, old Charlie, your benefactor, was conceived while Black Bob was away fighting the Boers in Africa, and there's many would swear he had the pure gauche of a granduncle of mine! If the gentry had kept to themselves, they'd have died out years ago! Every once in a while, you need a dollop of fresh blood, to add a bit of spine... a bit of spunk. I assure you, Mr. Hillman, that there's a bit of us in the best of them and a bit of them in the worst of us, 'tis nature's way! Have I shocked you, Mr Hillman?"

The question took me by surprise.

"I... a... "

"Are *you* married?" Another question, but one that I could answer.

"Divorced." I replied, with new confidence.

"Children?"

"No." Even as I answered, she tilted her head as though to X-ray me from another angle. Instantly, I could empathise with how stock bulls and prize stallions might feel.

"You might yet!" She almost smiled. "You're not in bad shape, what do you do?"

"I'm in banking."

"Rob Hillman!" She muttered, "*Rob...* a good name for a banker! By the way, your room won't be ready until tomorrow!" It wasn't an apology.

"I hadn't really thought..." I began, before recognizing an interim solution to my accommodation crisis. "But if you're sure it's not too much trouble..."

"Nothing, Mr Hillman, is too much trouble to a good housekeeper!" Again, her steely gaze, challenging... threatening... leaving me in no doubt that, regardless of whom the master of Ravenswood might be; she was mistress!

"Thank you, Mrs...?"

"Mrs. O! Will you be expecting an evening meal? I do have Fox to see to as well." It wasn't a question but nonetheless I felt obliged to answer.

"No, no thanks, I'm sure that I'll be able to make alternative arrangements." She was already on her feet, leading the way towards the porch. My audience was over; I was dismissed.

Back at the hotel, showered, shaved and still smarting, I savoured a last mouthful of coffee and decided that I deserved a cigar. The young barman was well rehearsed: even before I'd selected my cigar, he advised me that I could smoke in my bed-room, I could smoke in the street, I could smoke in the car park, but it was against the law to smoke my cigar within the public area of the hotel, and no, he did not stock matches.

I cheated. The aromatic flickering flames from the antique candelabra beside reception were just too tempting. Needing to exhale, I charged through the exit, almost colliding with a fellow outcast. My intended apology was stifled by the young woman's words.

"Mr Hillman, breaking the law already?" *Mr Hillman?* I thought turning to meet her quizzical grey gaze.

"Hello," I finally managed, "you have the advantage of me, have we met?"

"Claire Turner, we have now." I took her proffered hand; her grip was cool, firm and brief. "Let me explain, I'm a partner in your legal firm, it was I who traced you."

"Oh, in that case I'm in your debt, I owe you a drink... at least. How did you find me?" She blew a stream of smoke over her shoulder and treated me to a pearly smile.

"Well, as a native, I've always had an interest in the town's history and its people. When I was in London, a few years ago, I made a list of all the Hillmans in the phone book. Once I dis-covered that old Charlie's wish had been to trace his grandun-cle's descendants, I got busy on the phone... your ex-wife gave me your address."

"And here I am, thanks to both you and she."

"The lord of the manor, no less! Have you seen the place yet?"

"Yes, I made myself known this afternoon but the reception was somewhat cooler than I'd hoped for."

"Ah, you've met Mrs. O!"

"She's one tough old bird! Who – or what – is Fox?"

"Fox is a nickname, from his days as terrier man to the hunt. He's her husband, Jack Turner... my father!"

"Your *father*? So Mrs. O is...?"

"My mother!"

"Oh, I am so sorry, I meant no disrespect."

"None taken, she'd be thrilled with your description of her. She prides herself in being a battle-axe but, deep down, she's got a heart of gold!"

"But if your name is Turner, why is she called *Mrs. O?*"

"Her name is Olive, her predecessor was her mother-in-law, Bridget Turner, *Mrs. B!* The Turner line at Ravenswood is almost as long as the Hillman."

"So the next Hillman can expect a new set of Turners to tend to his needs?"

"You might be a nice guy, Mr. Hillman, but I don't see my brother and his wife leaving Harley Street to dig out foxes and cook breakfast for you. I've got to go, bye!" She took a final drag, crushed out her cigarette and pirouetted in a swirl of smoke and flowing dark hair. "And don't forget, you owe me a drink... at least!" She was gone.

"Bye!" I muttered as my eyes wandered towards a starry sky. Yes, tomorrow was already beginning to look a lot brighter.

Friday did start brightly. By ten o'clock, I was fed, packed, paid-up and checked out of the hotel but I had taken the precaution of booking a table for eight that evening. I was about to swing through the ivy-clad gate piers of Ravenswood when I remembered the Fiesta that I'd seen parked at the rear of the house on my previous visit. If that car could be driven straight to the door, so could mine. Galvanised by this logic, I continued past the entrance until I came to a crossroads. Taking a sharp left, I drove almost parallel to my previous route until something in my genetic memory clicked into gear and the car rattled over the cattle grid that guarded the rear entrance to my estate.

In total contrast to the impassable main avenue, this driveway was tarred and well maintained. Scattered stands of beech and oak kept watch over dense swathes of fading daffodils that peeped through long lines of weather-treated, wooden fencing. Soon, a little group of semi-detached Tudor cottages swung into view and, a few moments later, the functional side of Ravenswood House. A sudden clamour forced my attention back to my driving: flocks of hens, ducks and geese flapped, quacked and clucked their protestations at my intrusion. There was more to come.

Even as I parked beside the Fiesta, Mrs. O materialised in the doorway, her fists jammed aggressively against her hipbones.

"In this country, Mr. Hillman, livestock still have right of way on their own patch!"

"I'm sorry if I frightened your birds, I..."

"Oh, they're not mine; they're yours. Why should I bother with poultry when I've got free eggs? Well, don't just stand there, I should be seeing to Fox's lunch! I've stocked your fridge, you'll find a set of keys on the kitchen table!" She brushed past me, got into the Fiesta and drove off.

With Mrs. O now safely out of the way, I seized the opportunity to explore the house on my own. In addition to the cosy kitchen, the ground floor consisted of a large sitting room and a drawing room to the front, both well furnished and smelling strongly of wax polish. The floor also boasted a spacious dining room, complete with an impressive oak table and a dozen matching chairs. Opposite was a games room, equipped with snooker table, table tennis paraphernalia and several card tables. Facing the kitchen, a utility room housed a pantry, a large padlocked gun-safe and enough weatherproof gear to equip a small army. The hallway was dominated by an enormous hallstand, on which two huge black birds were perched, frozen in time beneath twin glass domes.

The first floor held a bathroom and four sizeable bedrooms, none of which was ready for occupation. I finally found my room on the second floor, overlooking the main entrance. It was larger than the other three on the top level, it was *en suite* and boasted a freshly dressed, king-sized bed. Behind a mesh screen, a turf fire glowed welcomingly in the ornate iron fireplace; perhaps Mrs. O did have a heart after all. Even my cursory glance at the generations of portraits that adorned every wall, stairway and landing brought Mrs. O's words to mind: I did look like one of them; the scary thing was that so did she!

My outdoor garb seemed to rejuvenate the old spaniel. Whirling in excited yapping circles, he pawed the gun-safe demandingly. Unconsciously, I appeased him by selecting a stout black-thorn from the array of walking sticks in an umbrella stand and ventured forth towards the verdant undulations beyond the stable block, the dog trotting contentedly at my heels. Once clear of the confines of the yard, the dog rolled back the years: his thumping bobbed tail, a rudder that zigzagged him through overgrown hedges and ditches. Intermittently, he would pause and lift his nose from a scent, to eye me with deferential curiosity. The animal's exuberance was contagious, I found myself studying the undergrowth and marvelling at the little splashes of colour that marked emerging bluebell, primrose and a host of other unidentified spring blooms.

I had no idea how far we had travelled when the dog came to an abrupt stop; his shoulders sloped, his neck stretched forward, his body rigid except for the frenzied flagging of his feathered stern. It took a few moments before I saw why: scarcely ten paces ahead, a brilliantly coloured cock pheasant peered uncertainly from the almost perfect camouflage of last year's bracken.

"Send him in, sir!" The deep male voice came from the other side of the hedge.

"Go on, boy!" I ventured.

"*Flush*! Tell him to flush, sir!" continued my phantom advisor.

"Flush!" I obeyed. The dog sprang forward, sending the bird like a whirring crowing arrow towards the opposite corner of the field. The spaniel eyed me expectantly until a loud handclap from beyond the boundary triggered him to an enthusiastic pursuit of the fleeing pheasant.

"He'll sleep after that, sir!" My mentor continued. I took a few steps towards a partial gap in the thorn fence and found myself face-to-face with a medium sized, middle-aged man, attired in a green waxed jacket and matching flat cap.

"Rob Hillman!" I stretched my hand between sprigs of haw-thorn.

"I'm pleased to make your acquaintance, sir; Jack Turner, but better known as *Fox*! The wind is rising; it could be a big one. I thought the horses would be safer indoors. Besides, this old lady is nearly due." He patted the neck of the chestnut mare that I'd seen on my first visit. Two younger bay coloured animals pranced around in loose skittish arcs.

"Good to meet you too, Jack." I found myself squirming through a gap in the fence.

"Why don't you have any halters on the horses?"

"The young ones have never even had a head collar on and this old girl doesn't need one. Where she goes, they'll follow; she's their mother... the Punchestown winner!" His fingers scratched the mare's pink muzzle. "Can you whistle, sir?"

"What?" I whirled in surprise.

"If you don't call that old dog back, he'll be hunting that rooster 'til morning! Old Charlie had a sort of curlew whistle; try it, sir!" Eventually, despairing of my futile attempts to impersonate Charlie's signal, Fox relented and whistled the spaniel to heel. I fell into step with Fox and, chatting easily, we angled towards Ravenswood House, the animals following quietly in our wake.

Fox knew his weather, I decided, struggling to steer a straight course past the Fiesta, which was now parked at the Tudor cottage nearest the road. If anything, the wind seemed to have increased in intensity and, as I neared the town, my dipped headlights grew increasingly ineffective against the premature evening gloom.

The hotel was a hive of activity, the mound of fishing equipment by the reception area bore testament to the popularity of the forthcoming event. Despite the extra demands on his time, the hotel manager ushered me towards a tiny corner table in the dining room. Seeing that the table was already occupied, I hesitated until a pair of grey eyes twinkled at me... her mother's eyes... my eyes...

"Claire?" I finally managed. "What a surprise, may I join you?" She treated me to the full benefit of her smile.

"Of course, it's your table... I've had to promise to vacate it on your arrival. It's all yours now!" She started to rise.

"No, please stay... I..."

"Thanks, but I really must go, I'm secretary of the anglers' association, so I have to register the entries. Would you be available to present a trophy tomorrow evening?"

"Me? Of course... but why?"

"The competition takes place on your river and you are the main sponsor, that's why!"

"I'll be here! What about that drink... at least...?" I was pleading.

"Oh, I fully intend to hold you to that... tomorrow! *Bon appetite, Mr. Hillman!*"

I don't remember much about that meal; I just sort of slipped into a trance until jolted back to reality by the ferocity of the elements as I dashed back to the sanctuary of my car. Fox's weather forecast had been right on the money. I reached Ravenswood without mishap and, remembering Fox's advice, decided to consign my car to the safety of one of the coach houses. After much heaving, I finally forced the double doors sufficiently along their rusting rollers to allow entry for my car.

It was then I saw it: in the beam of my headlights, beneath a shroud of dusty green tarpaulin, reposed the unmistakable lines of a classic vintage automobile. With trembling fingers, I lifted the cover and gasped. Although an Aston Martin had been my dream, I could live with the consolation of the white E Type Jaguar that now stood before me, its twin black leather seats just as pristine as the day it had left the showroom. A loud splintering crash sounded somewhere in the darkness beyond; just the nudge I needed to seek the protection of the house, a good book and a warm bed.

It was the birdsong that woke me shortly after dawn. Pulling back the drapes to bright sunlight, I stretched and blinked in disbelief at my first sight of the distant ocean. Fascinated, I dressed hurriedly and charged across the yard. The explanation was soon evident: the huge Macrocarpa cypress that had dominated the skyline had fallen victim to the gales, perhaps causing the very crash that I'd heard from the coach house.

The calls rang clear in the still air - *pruck, pruck, pruck* - I glanced upward and, thanks to my late night perusal of Charlie's nature books, could now distinguish the lofty dark shapes from the lesser rooks and jackdaws that strove to repair their damaged nests: the ravens *were* still here. It was then I noticed another casualty of the storm; the little summerhouse that had stood in the clearing behind the ill-fated tree had been struck by a trailing limb and reduced to a scattering of rubble.

Tiptoeing through the ruins, I almost tripped over a rusting metal box. Fascinated, I prised it open. From my average banker's knowledge of legal documents, I instantly realised that I had succeeded where Charlie had failed: thanks to an old pine tree and a gust of wind, I had stumbled upon Black Bob's hiding place.

"She's foaled! It's a colt, sir... he's a beauty; we should keep him!" Even from across the yard, Fox's excitement was infectious.

"Of course we will, Jack!" I heard myself reply. After all, I was in possession of the deeds of Ravenswood: it was mine to do with as I pleased... I could sense bigger decisions looming but my immediate priority was to meet with an intriguing young lady... for a drink... at least...

DRIVEN

"Are you going out tonight?" Betty asked, her back against the kitchen sink, her hands clasped beneath her damp tea towel.

"Why?" She jerked involuntarily at her husband's barked monosyllable and began to wipe an already dried plate.

"I've got my class this evening and... "

"Your class? What's the point of you taking car maintenance classes anyway? It's a waste of time and money. By the way, my car insurance is due next month; that's what you should be thinking about, not bloody classes!" Deeming the discussion over, Dom drained his mug and thumbed the volume button of the TV remote control.

"Is there any more tea?" He half-shouted without removing his eyes from the screen. Betty took a deep breath before refilling his mug and, mustering her courage, forced the question between quivering lips.

"Will you be able to give something towards the insurance?"

"Me? Hah, that's a good one! Insurance is a household bill, just like the telephone and electricity! Why do you think I give you housekeeping money, woman?" With a further guffaw, Dom sprang to his feet and stormed from the house. Betty returned to the kitchen and, sighing resignedly, struck a number of less-essential items from her shopping list.

Betty reached her class with seconds to spare. During her twenty-minute walk through the rainy November night, she found herself assessing, yet again, her quarter-century of married life. While Dom could have never been described as generous, he had – in the past – made occasional grudging contributions towards some of the larger annual expenses. Back then, they still clung to the dream of a family but, since Betty's menopause, all semblance of a partnership had vanished.

After her class, the worsening weather forced Betty to impose upon her elder sister for a drive home.

"Just get out, leave him! Mum's granny flat is free and you earn enough to live comfortably on your own. You'll always be welcome here!" Jane announced as she freshened her sister's teacup.

"I appreciate all that but I'm not ready to fill a dead woman's shoes, just yet!"

"You should at least have a car of your own. I mean, damn it all, you had a car ever before you met him. It really bugs me having to watch you trudging the roads like a poor scholar, while he's swanking around that Mercedes!"

"I know but... No, it's not worth the hassle."

"But, Betty, a *Mercedes*, I ask you! Fair enough, your mortgage is paid but what does he want a Mercedes for? You could easily afford to run two ordinary cars for what that thing must be costing!"

It was after lunch on the following Sunday that Betty reopened the subject.

"Dom, I've been thinking..."

"Humph?" He shrugged, adjusting his stockinged feet on the armrest of the couch.

"I was thinking, now that the mortgage is paid off, perhaps I... maybe... we could afford a second car?" she paused, bracing herself for an outburst.

"What about the car?" he asked distractedly.

"No, not your car... maybe it's time we got a second car. It wouldn't have to be new or anything... just..."

"Are my ears deceiving me, you want a car all to yourself? Good Christ, woman; have you any idea what it costs to run a car these days?"

"But I wouldn't have to be borrowing yours all the time and now that the mortgage..."

"This is your sister's doing, isn't it? What do you need a car for anyway? Your work is only five minute's walk down the road. For Christ's sake, woman, most people can't even find parking that close to their job! I'm the one who has to drive up and down the bloody country every day. Besides, my car is there for you whenever you want it."

"But it isn't. Most of the time I..."

"It's there for you right now. Here, take the keys, go on!" He threw the keys onto the table before her. "All you have to do is put some juice into it!"

"But I don't want the car tonight, I..."

"Well, if you're not going out; I will. It's plain I'll get no peace here tonight!"

After breakfast, on the following Saturday, Dom returned to the subject of cars.

"I want you to take the Merc over to Joe Mac; there's a rattle under the bonnet."

"A rattle, what kind of a rattle?"

"I don't know, it's a rattle; he'll know!"

"Are you not golfing today?"

"Paul is picking me up but I will want the car back here before six. Pay him whatever it costs and get an invoice... just make sure that it's blank!"

"Maybe I could take a look at it first, maybe I...!"

"What? You want to go fiddling with my Mercedes? Hah, in your dreams, woman! Take it over to Joe Mac, there's some chance he might know what he's doing!"

It took less than ten minutes for Joe Mac to confirm Betty's diagnosis. After a few quick turns of a ratchet, the powerful engine purred just as sweetly as it had on its first test-drive.

"Betty, if you ever feel like a career change, give me a shout. I could really use somebody with your instincts around here!" The mechanic wiped his hands on the seat of his overalls before closing the hood of the Mercedes. Betty rewarded him with the ghost of a distracted smile; her attention was focussed on the other side of the yard.

"How much would that little yellow one cost?"

"The *Clio*? Are you interested?"

"I don't know... maybe... "

"Thirty-four K on the clock; good tyres; nearly two-years NCT; taxed until March; regularly serviced; one owner... you know her... Mrs Ryan... the teacher. To you I'd say four... am four... no... four even... and, I'll throw in a full service when it's due. I'll get the keys; take her for a spin!"

"Ah no, I don't know. Maybe some other time? I really should be going. What do I owe you? Oh, and can you do an invoice for him, please? You know..."

"I know, but for once, I going to make more out of the job than he will! Is that all right with you?" They shook conspiratorially. "And, Betty, if you're serious about buying a car, come to me first; I'll see you right!"

On her return home, it was clear that Dom's fourball hadn't gone well.

"Is the car done?" His voice sounded from the kitchen. By way of an answer, she handed him the invoice. Her only thanks was a grunt as he slipped the paper into his briefcase.

"I was looking at a car today, at Joe Mac's, he wanted me to take it for..."

"You're not still going on about that! This is Jane's doing, isn't it? It's all very well for Bobby and Jane to have their cars. Oh yeah, they have it all, and they got it for nothing! He walked straight from college into the family business, the biggest bloody haulage company in the county at that! And, who got your mother's house? Bloody Jane!"

"But it was Jane who cared for mother when..."

"They've never had to worry about mortgages; they've never had to worry about anything... born with bloody silver spoons, the pair of them. I don't want to hear any more about cars!" Swiping his keys from the coffee table, he stormed into the hallway.

"You're not going out again, are you? Dinner is nearly..." her words ended with a frustrated sigh as the front door slammed shut.

That evening, after Mass, Betty called to Jane and told her about the yellow car.

"That's a great deal, go for it! Marian Ryan treated that car like a baby!"

"I know but..."

"If it's the money..."

"No, I have the money, it's…"

"It's just that *he* doesn't know that you have it?"

"He'd have a fit if he thought I had that kind of money," she giggled girlishly for a moment, then sobered as another thought struck her. "By God, he'd never give me another penny house-keeping!"

"Will you listen to yourself? Does that sound like some-one who is respected and feared by burly truckers all over Europe? You're basically running our business, I might sign the paycheques but, as far as the lads are concerned, you're the boss! Even Bobby wouldn't dare question your decisions, and still you let Dom walk all over you. That's it, I should have thought of it before!" Jane was on her feet, her outstretched hands gripping Betty's shoulders. "We'll buy that car for you, or whatever car you like. You deserve a company car anyway, you've earned it!"

"No, no… I mean thanks… but no thanks, I couldn't! He already resents the relationship that I have with you… both of you… No, there has to be another way… there just has to be…"

During her lunch-break on Monday, Betty visited her insurance broker and, having renewed the cover on the Mercedes, digested the additional data that the assistant had supplied to her. The answer was there in plain black and white, it wasn't just her best option; it was her only one. For a further fortnight she agonised over her decision, but the more she thought about it and, the more soakings she suffered going about her daily business, the more determined she became to see it through.

The weather was particularly foul on the evening of Betty's next class. December's arrival was opaqued behind bitter easterly gusts that drove scything sheets of hail before each strengthening squall. Despite her hours of pleading on the previous evening, Dom had been unrelenting: her class was not going to interfere with his agenda, he would be watching the international match between six and eight and the golf club AGM was timed for eight-thirty. Jane's offer of a lift to the college presented a partial solution but, as Jane had commitments afterwards, Betty had reluctantly booked a TAXI for the journey home.

The cab's arrival coincided with the wailing of the first siren. The ambulance was closely followed by a fire engine, which seemed to tow a convoy of Garda cars in its slipstream.

"This looks serious!" The driver whistled, lowering his window.

"I sincerely hope it's not as bad as it sounds..." Betty said, fastening her seat belt. A few moments later, a grim-faced young Garda waved their vehicle to a halt, explaining that there had been an accident at the bad bend, just ahead.

"We could be here for a while!" the driver muttered and reached for his cigarette packet. "Do you mind, Betty?"

"I might, unless you offer me one!" she answered, reaching her open palm towards him.

They had both finished their second cigarettes when the Garda finally gave them the signal to proceed.

"Christ, that doesn't look good!" The driver observed as the ambulance approached them, blue lights flashing but sirens ominously silent. For several moments afterwards, the only sound Betty could hear was that of her own heart thumping against her ribcage. Double-checking the rear registration plate of the mangled Mercedes car, she sighed and wondered whether Dom might have finally conceded that Betty's motor maintenance classes hadn't been a waste after all...

THE POWER

"I suppose ye'll be getting the power in?" Shattering the companionable silence, Tom's guttural tone reverberated around the tiny kitchen. Momentarily startled, Jimmy looked up from his usual stone perch, inside Tom's open chimneystack. Jimmy took a deep breath, glad of the distraction from his futile attempts to carve something resembling a pig from a sod of hard black turf. Tom was a genius with his great big shovels of hands, he could fashion any animal you'd name from the unwieldy material and then just casually throw the exquisitely detailed effigy onto the open fire.

"What's the power, Tom?" Tom blinked in amusement and chuckled, revealing the few remaining yellow teeth that had survived well over a half-century of hardship and neglect.

"The power is a wondrous thing, a truly wondrous thing, entirely." If Jimmy had expected a more detailed explanation, he was disappointed. Yet, despite the natural curiosity of a seven-year-old, Jimmy knew better than to attempt to force the issue. Tom would talk when he wanted to talk but, other than that, neither God nor man could squeeze a single word out of the gentle giant. Resignedly, Jimmy renewed his efforts at creativity, sighing with frustration each time he drove the penknife too deep and a potential head or leg dropped to the caked mud of the cabin floor.

Too soon, the dusk of the early March evening crept in. The sound of a safety match being struck was Jimmy's cue to depart. Tom was thrifty with his matches: most days he used only one, first lighting the mirror oil-lamp that sat on the deep sill of the room's only window, before applying the flame to his first pipe of the day. Any subsequent smokes would be reddened by a succession of embers from the ever-smouldering turf fire. Tom took a few deep puffs from his black briar and settled stiffly back onto his rickety *súgán* chair, the only conventional seat in the house. Jimmy took one last regretful look at his latest failure before tossing it into the warm glow of the open hearth. A little shower of sparks rose and then extinguished against the blackened iron kettle that continuously hung from its hook on the soot-encrusted crane.

"Are you away, young Jimmy? Safe home to you." Tom returned the pipe to his mouth, his features contorting as he forced distant teeth together in a vain attempt to gain a controlling grip on the pipe-stem.

"Good luck, Tom. I'll see you tomorrow." Jimmy departed through the open half-door with Tom's reflective mutterings yielding to the territorial warbling of a roosting blackbird.

"Ah yeah, a truly wondrous thing, entirely..."

The kitchen of Jimmy's house was a world away from the one he had just left. The room was bathed in a soft warm glow from the gently hissing Tilley lamp that hung from the centre of the ceiling, a gleaming silver kettle whistled urgently on the polished black Stanley range and, most importantly of all, a freshly-baked apple pie waited invitingly in the centre of the prepared supper table. Jimmy rushed towards his usual seat between his father and his sister only to have his progress halted by a question from his mother.

"Did you wash your hands?" She spooned tealeaves into the scalded pot.

"They're clean, look!" Jimmy presented both sides of his hands for inspection.

"They can't be. God only knows what you could pick up in that house. Go out and wash them... Now!" Knowing the futility of further argument, Jimmy retreated to the yard and solemnly rubbed his palms together in the icy water of the rain barrel that stood beneath the gable eaves' chute. The onerous chore completed, he resumed his place at the table and crossed himself just as devoutly as his sister had earlier done.

Hunger took precedence over curiosity until a lightly boiled egg and several slices of soda bread had been consumed and only a few scattered crumbs remained to testify to the palatability of the contents of the enamel baking plate.

"Are we getting the power?" Jimmy took a gulp of tea and waited, more in hope than in expectation, for an adult to respond.

"Who was talking about the power?" Dad asked.

"Tom was, he asked me if we'd be getting it."

"Is Tom getting it?" Mum seemed strangely amused at her own question.

"I suppose... What...?"

"Yeah, we'll be taking it all right." Dad topped up his mug from the cosy-covered teapot.

"It'll be a pure blessing, may the Lord hasten the day!" Mum seemed to be warming to the subject.

"Can I have a hairdryer?" Jimmy allowed himself a fleeting grin at Breda's question. *Typical girl.* He thought; comforted by the knowledge that his sister had no idea what they were talking about.

"Humph!" Jimmy's grin broadened. *Well done, Dad. That's telling her.*

"Look, it's early days. We'll have to see." It seemed that Mum was almost as confused as Breda. Clearly, the power must be a man-thing. Jimmy resolved to have another go at Tom after school next evening.

Much to his disappointment, Jimmy was forced to put his plan on hold. There was no sign of Tom when he called on the morrow. Mum expressed her surprise at seeing her son engrossed in arithmetic at four o'clock on a Friday afternoon.

"Tom's not there." Was the boy's downcast response.

"Oh, he's probably away ploughing somewhere. I saw him heading off, with the horse, early this morning." That explained it, Jimmy had no choice but to wait; or did he? The answer to his burning question came from an unlikely source: Breda.

It was teatime and there was still no sign of Tom returning to base. Emerging from her room after completing her homework, Breda sighed, rubbing her eyes wearily.

"Oh, janey, if the power doesn't come soon, I'll be gone completely blind." Her words were directed at nobody in particular.

Jimmy waited for a parental comment; there was none. Perhaps he should say something.

"Why?" Breda whirled in surprise, as if noticing Jimmy for the first time.

"Because, silly, when the power comes, we'll be able to have the electric light in every room." Her words were laden with the type of disdain that sisters reserve specifically for younger male siblings. Jimmy digested the news in muted triumph. So that was it; that's what the power was all about. His very own house was going to have switches and wires and bulbs, just like they had in the new school. Now, he really had something to tell Tom.

The meal was well over when the slow heavy clip-clop of Tom's grey mare rang out on the paved passage outside Jimmy's bedroom. His jigsaw puzzle instantly forgotten, the boy charged into the kitchen. Dad flashed a warning glare from his leaning position beside the crackling speaker of the *Pye* radio set on the sideboard. Mum and sister both glanced up from their knitting. Jimmy took a deep steadying breath before presenting his hushed petition to his mother.

"Can I go down to Tom? I won't be long. All my lessons are done and... and tomorrow is Saturday. Can I? ... Can I, Mum? Can I... please?" Mum cast a raised eye in Dad's direction, Dad glanced at the pendulum clock above the chimneybreast, Breda's jaw dropped in horror at her parents' delay in refusing such an outrageous request.

"It's dark." She turned appealingly from one parent to the other.

"Yeah." Dad's intervention brought only brief hope to the twelve-year-old. "Breda is right, you'd better take the lamp." Breda was in for an even bigger shock from her mother.

"Ask Tom to come up for a bit of supper. He's been away all day and that old fire of his is probably gone out. I'll throw something together here for him."

The bicycle-lamp was taken but not required. Whether in light or dark, each bump and hollow of Tom's cart-rutted passage was as familiar to Jimmy as the undulations of the patchwork quilt on his own bed. The little house was in silent darkness. Jimmy's ears guided him to the lean-to that served as both byre and stable, where the beam of his lamp revealed the docile shire mare happily munching oats from a tin basin, while Tom wiped her withers dry with a handful of jute sacking.

"That light will blind us!" After a quick turn of Jimmy's fingers, night was restored.

"Ye were away ploughing, Tom?"

"That we were, *garsún*, across at Pa Lynch's. We could be there for another week." Tom replied without breaking rhythm.

"Tom. We're getting the power all right and... and the light!" Tom's chuckle came through the blackness, Jimmy could visualise the gleam of mirth in the pale grey eyes.

"Ah yeah, the power is a wondrous thing, to be sure. I well remember when I was working for the Red Sullivans, back behind Killaderry..."

"Wasn't that where you saw the deer, Tom, stags as big as giraffes, with antlers as wide as a hay cart?" Dancing from one foot to the other, Jimmy stretched his arms to their maximum. "Tell me about the deer, Tom."

"Ah yeah, the deer were the boyos, Jimmy, they..."

"They could jump like *Arkle* and, once they got their tails up, not *Brian Ború* nor *Finn Mac Cool* or even *Ronnie Delaney* himself could keep up with them, isn't that right, Tom?"

"That's right, Jimmy; no matter what kind of a fence we'd put up; we couldn't keep 'em out of the corn. A pure heart-scald it was to go out in the morning and see your months of work just trampled into the ground. We even stayed up all night but no good. The deer were the boyos, they could see us but we couldn't see 'em. The deer is a wondrous boyo, all right, a truly wondrous boyo. I'll tell you, Jimmy, 'twas no joke milking a herd of thirty cows after spending a night chasing deer. Torture it was, sheer torture. I was on the point of hitting for England when the power came. I'd heard tell of the milking machine from a cousin who'd worked in the midlands but his stories didn't do it justice. What a pleasure it was to rig it up and listen to the *pish-pish*, *pish-pish* of the milk hitting the froth in the buckets and to hear the clusters sucking all four teats at the one time. I didn't know myself, *garsún*, watching that machine, morning and evening, and me puffing my pipe to my heart's content. Ah, the power is a wondrous thing, to be sure, a truly..."

"My mother says you're to come up for your supper; she's throwing something together for you."

"A wondrous woman, your mother; ah yeah, truly wondrous woman, entirely. Off you go and tell her that I'll be up as soon as I finish here with Molly."

Almost a half-hour had passed before the latch of the back door was finally lifted.

"Hello, the house!" Muttering something about *atmospherics*, Dad switched the whistling wails of the radio to silence.

"Is it yourself, Tom? Come in and welcome!"

"God bless all here!" Tom replied as Breda headed to her room with a disgruntled sigh. Jimmy pushed his chair closer to the table as Mum called out from the kitchen.

"And you too, sir! Come in to the table." Tom hung his grimy tweed cap on a rusting cup hook as he closed the door.

"Thanks and 'tis awful good of you, Missus, awful good, entirely..." Tom seated himself on Breda's abandoned chair, self-consciously smoothing the few silver hairs that intruded across his glistening dome.

"Yerra sure, it's only a bit of stuff that I had left over from the dinner." As she placed a plate of steaming bacon omelette before her guest, a sideways glance ensured that her son's un-asked questions dissolved before his lips could shape the words. Jimmy propped his elbows on the table and, resigned to an interlude of enforced silence, cupped his chin in his upturned palms. As he watched Tom butter a thick wedge of soda bread, the boy idly wondered if the visitor's calloused hands had encountered any water since they had finished grooming the mare.

Tom wiped his plate clean with a surviving heel-end of bread and drained his mug with ill-disguised relish. Replete, Tom clasped his hands together behind his poll and stretched back on the cushioned dining chair, powerful muscles rippling inside his collarless off-white shirt. Jimmy's rising hopes of further tales of the power were dashed when Dad pounced to pick Tom's brain on the merits of various varieties of seed potatoes. On-and-on the men talked, until the pendulum clock chimed nine times. Jimmy looked appealingly at Mum; she smiled benignly but there was no doubting the resolve behind the firm shake of her head. Reluctantly, Jimmy said his goodnights and retreated to his bedroom. Sleep came swiftly and brought with it count-less adventures with ancient Celtic heroes (all of whom looked remarkably like Tom) leading the charge on great white horses, against marauding hoards of bloodthirsty antlered invaders.

On Monday, Jimmy arrived home from school to find Mum in a frenzied tizzy. Perplexingly, her usually pristine kitchen was in anarchic disarray. Hammers, saws, chisels and pliers were everywhere. Sawdust and mortar littered the unswept concrete floor: the wiring for the power had begun.

Uncle Jack, who had worked in England and knew about the power, seemed to be directing operations from somewhere above the newly-cut square hole in the ceiling. Inexplicably, Dad appeared to have assumed the mantle of servant in his own home, bustling to and fro in response to each muffled command from above. Suddenly, Jack's grime-encrusted face materialised from the darkened beyond; Mum glared up at her brother.

"What is it now?"

"Did I hear young Jimmy? I was thinking that if he's home you might be making a cup of tea." The petitioner's eyes blinked uncertainly.

"Oh, all right then, come on down. Jimmy, shove the kettle onto the hotplate and tell your father... and then, why don't you run down to Tom for a while?"

"Tom is away ploughing; I'll stay here and..."

"Oh, very well; one more child won't make much difference around the place." With trembling hands, she buttered thick wedges of maize-meal bread.

The chaos continued for most of that week. During the ex-citement of the wiring, Jimmy was far too preoccupied to even think of visiting Tom. Each day at school, he exchanged progress reports with his classmates; each night, his dreams were filled with the voices of his father and uncle and their whole new vocabulary. Words like: cables, switches, sockets, plugs, fuses and junction boxes spun around the ceilings like hunted bluebottles and, if all that wasn't enough, First Communion was just around the corner.

As it happened, the First Communion was to arrive before the power. Mother was in a tizzy again but all the shopping, measuring, scrubbing and grooming was worthwhile. Jimmy arrived home that evening showing a profit of nearly a whole fiver: two one-pound notes, two ten-shilling notes and almost another two pounds in change. He was rich. Once back home, with all the fuss and bustle of the occasion over, the boy realised how long it had been since he had seen Tom. He simply had to go and tell him all the news. After a quick change of clothes, he set off.

Tom shielded his eyes against the setting watery sun, as the familiar navy-blue woollen jersey flashed between the blooming gorse bushes that skirted the passage to his home.

"Tom, I made my First Communion and got a pile of money!" Jimmy called out from a distance. Tom waved encouragingly and disappeared indoors. Moments later, as Jimmy rounded the final bend; Tom's welcome rang out from within.

"What's keeping you, *garsún*, come in and tell me all about it!" Jimmy promptly obliged, hardly pausing for breath until he noticed that Tom's kitchen showed no signs of being prepared for the power.

"Tom...?"

"Ah well, you must have had a wondrous day, *garsún*; a truly wondrous day, entirely!"

"Tom, where are your wires... for the plugs and the lights and things?" The question was greeted with a tolerant chuckle.

"Ah sure, what would I be wanting the like of them things for?" A terrible thought crossed Jimmy's mind. Mum had complained about the cost of getting the power in; what if Tom was unable to meet the expense of it all?

"But, Tom, I have the money if you want it. I made..." Another chuckle.

"You're a good boy, Jimmy. The power will be a great thing for your family but I'm too set in my ways to go changing things around now. By the way, I have a present for you... for your First Communion. One minute and I'll get it." Tom opened the door that led to his only other room and emerged moments later with a box that could have easily accommodated Dad's wellingtons. Tom placed the box in Jimmy's outstretched hands.

"Thanks, Tom, but what is it?"

"It's an electric reading lamp ... for you bedroom. The man behind Killaderry gave it to me when I was leaving; you'll be able to use it when you have the power."

The big day was approaching fast; the power would soon be turned on. Fragile looking glass bulbs were fitted to the wires that protruded from the holes in the ceiling, a special red one was placed on a bracket before the big picture of *The Sacred Heart* and stern warnings were issued about the dangers of sticking matches, nails or fingers into the inviting holes in the wall sockets. Then it happened; in an instant, the power began to flow. The shadowy ghosts of the night were banished forever, as brilliant light flooded every nook and cranny of the house and Tom's reading lamp beamed proudly down on Jimmy's pillow. There was a downside too, however, and those who suffered most were the spiders... and Dad. Web-spinning dynasties that had flourished for generations in blissful semi-gloom were now cruelly highlighted and subjected to Mum's unrelenting crusade of eviction or death.

Once the spiders had been vanquished, Dad was browbeaten into painting every room, from ceiling to skirting board, until Jimmy had to concede that Tom might have a point after all. Meanwhile, hardly a month went by without the introduction of another new gadget to further baffle the bewildered household, until finally, in September, the huge box appeared inside the scullery door.

The latest arrival was obviously of great importance; it was the only item that Mum had got seriously excited over since peace had been restored after the spider and painting campaigns. Breda was equally ecstatic because, whatever was in the big box, it had brought a free hair dryer with it. Uncle Jack had to be sent for to hook up the new wonder machine and was presented with tea immediately on his arrival. The cardboard was removed to reveal yet another box, a white box with a door in the bottom half and one missing in the top. As Jack completed his operation, Jimmy was still none the wiser. He scanned the adult faces in the vain hope of finding one that might be someway receptive to yet another silly question.

"Isn't it lovely?" Breda's words gave him new hope.

"It is; what is it?"

"It's a hairdryer, silly!" Haughtily shaking her head, she consigned her prize to the safety of her room before following her parents into the yard to wave a thankful farewell to Uncle Jack.

Finding himself alone and unsupervised and with the strange new object at his mercy, Jimmy decided to find out exactly why Mum should be so absorbed with such a plain looking item. He studied it for a moment, noting the four black discs on the top and the row of numbered dials on its face. He turned a dial and waited for something to happen. Nothing. He turned another with a similar result; he turned the rest of them, still nothing. More perplexed than ever, he wandered towards the yard as Breda was coming back in. Moments later, her scream brought both parents scurrying back from the gate.

"Mum, he's been at your new cooker, all the rings are red-hot; it's wasting all the units!" So, that's what it was!

Time seemed to pass more quickly after that. Soon, a new electric radio was installed in the kitchen and Jimmy helped Dad deliver the old *wet-and-dry-battery* model to Tom's grateful possession. The onset of winter meant long evenings of reading and radio plays and, when Christmas dawned, Breda was granted yet another wish as a new record player took pride of place in the revamped parlour.

As the new year aged, Jimmy's visits to Tom grew even less frequent. The twin lures of the school football team and the wonders of the public library meant that he was spending more of his time in the town. Whenever Tom was called to assist with a difficult calving or some other emergency, he would comment on the boy's growth rate and make gentle enquires as to how school was progressing.

Jimmy was twelve when the television set arrived, amid a wave of expectation reminiscent of the advent of the power itself. By now, Dad had overcome his fear of all things electrical and was determined to be master in his own house again. Jimmy was thrilled at his own elevation in rank; his would be the crucial job of monitoring the snowy screen and shouting up to Dad, who was in the attic, whenever a shadowy St. Bridget's Cross would flicker into view. It truly was a mind-boggling undertaking, but within a few hours the whole family was seated in awe-filled anticipation before the magic box. Soon a lady's voice spluttered through the eerie silence, followed by that first ghostly face that wavered in and out of focus as the news headlines were relayed over the airwaves.

"It's better than the radio." Jimmy was first to break the spell.

"It's not as good as the television in the convent." Breda was less enthusiastic.

"It's the atmospherics." There was a note of finality in Dad's words.

"Shush!" Mum's hissed command had the desired effect on her household.

It was over a month later that Jimmy found himself at odds with Breda again.

"I think we should invite Tom to watch the All-Ireland football final with us."

"No way, I don't want that stinking old man in this house!"

"Breda! That's no way to talk about Tom; he's been a great neighbour to us!"

"But, Dad! He... he's dirty and his pipe makes me sick."

"Your father is right, child." Mum concurred, "Tom has been a good friend... as well as a great neighbour."

"You don't even like football! Anyway, you'll be playing your records or out with your..." Jimmy was encouraged by the way the exchanges were going.

"*Jimmy!* Mum, make him stop, please!"

"Jimmy!"

"Maybe he's right, *a stór*. Breda, you've never watched a football match!"

"But, Dad, we've never had a television until now!"

"We had it for the semi-final and you still went out with ..."

"*Mu-um!*"

"*Jimmy!*"

"All right, all right!" Three pairs of eyes turned to Dad. "Jimmy, run down and ask Tom if he'd like to come for his lunch on Sunday."

Tom's arrival coincided with the start of the minor match. Breda had already retreated to the parlour and the record player, while Mum was putting the finishing touches to the meal in the scullery. From the outset, Jimmy suspected that his guest was less than enthralled with the new apparatus.

"It's the atmospherics," Jimmy volunteered in the absence of Dad, who had gone to change from his Sunday suit to his regular clothes.

"Where's the aerial?" Tom whispered, easing out of his chair as Jimmy raised his eyes towards the ceiling. "Come on, *garsún*, quick!" Tom was now directly underneath the manhole. "Come on, I'll lift you up!" Jimmy found himself being effortlessly hoisted by powerful arms. "Go on, push it up!" Tom urged. "Can you see the aerial? Can you twist the pole? Go on, I'll tell you when to stop... Good... a bit more... Stop! Come down, quick!" Both were seated before Dad returned to the room.

"If 'twould only stay like that." Dad sighed, stooping to inspect the sharpened images on the screen. "It's the atmospherics, you see..."

Ten years later, Breda did watch the final, together with Mum and Tom and baby Seán. Dad wasn't with them for that one; he was in Croke Park, watching Jimmy – and Breda's husband John – help bring the All-Ireland title back to the county for the first time in over a quarter-century.

It was in the following spring that Jimmy came home for the Christening of Breda's daughter. All through supper, he had the disturbing feeling that Mum had something on her mind. It was only when Dad had gone out to have a final look at a heifer that was due to calve that she finally spoke her mind.

"You should go down to see Tom; he's been asking about you a lot lately. I'm a bit worried about him, he... he looks fine but it's not like him to keep going on so much about anything, maybe he'll talk to you..."

With a heavy heart, Jimmy retraced the footsteps of his boyhood. Was Tom seriously ill? What age would he be now? Jimmy felt a surge of shame at the sight of the overgrown brambles along the passage; he should have made more of an effort to keep in contact. He paused and watched the thin wisp of blue smoke emerge from the chimney behind the pole... The pole? Yes, there was a pole: a new electricity pole, standing proudly, mid-way along the passage. Tom had finally got the power. Jimmy broke into a trot, the cool evening air filling his lungs. He resisted the urge to call out before reaching the open door. A naked bulb glowed welcomingly in the empty kitchen.

"Tom? Tom, are you at home? It's me... Jimmy." There was no reply from within. Jimmy called out again, his eyes scanning the room for any further improvements the power might have brought to Tom's primitive existence. There were none: no fridge or cooker, no electric kettle, no television or radio, not even a wall socket. Except for the solitary bulb, nothing had changed since fifteen years before. Then Jimmy heard it, it was faint at first but once he stepped outside of the house, he had no doubt; someone was calling his name. Had something happened to Tom? Had he fallen?

"Tom, Tom, where are you, Tom? It's me... Jimmy!"

"I'm here, *garsún*; in the stall. Come in and see for yourself!" Jimmy rounded the corner to the lean-to door and peered inside. At first he could see nothing; slowly, Tom's kneeling figure seemed to materialise out of the gloom.

"Tom, are you all right, Tom?" Tom's chuckle was as infectious as ever.

"Am I all right, young Jimmy? You may say that I'm all right." A giant hand motioned Jimmy forward. "Look at this, *garsún,* look!" At that, Jimmy heard the click of a switch, just as Tom's head became silhouetted against a great crimson halo. "Look, Jimmy!" Edging forward, Jimmy followed the pointing finger to where a pair of fluffy fox cubs lapped contentedly from Tom's frying pan. "About a month ago, I heard 'em *olagóning* in the wood. Their eyes were closed and they were wet and cold, trying to suckle from their dead mother. Only for I buying that red lamp, they'd have been gonners, entirely." Grinning toothlessly, he rubbed his palms together beneath the glowing bulb. "Ah, *garsún,* the power is a wondrous thing, ah yeah; a truly wondrous thing, entirely..."

Community Service

"Go on, ask her!" His mouth shielded by his left palm, Mick Nevin's right elbow nudged at his brother's ribs.

"*You* ask her. It's *you* that..." Matt hissed, tired of the weekly ritual.

"Go on, it isn't as if you'd be asking for yourself. Quick, she's going!"

"She's gone!" Matt grinned, draining the dregs of his stout. "It's your round." He craned his neck and eyeballed his sibling. "Well? I bought last!" Abruptly, Mick got to his feet and pushed himself back from the bar.

"You call it, I'll be back in a minute..." Without further explanation, Mick hurried towards the door, Matt's bemused eyes following each lopsided step.

The drinks arrived as Mick slowly resumed his seat.

"Well?" Matt ventured before taking a long swallow from his fresh pint. "*Sláinte!*"

"*Sláinte!* No good, I'll have to wait until someone drops out."

"Or drops off!" Matt chuckled softly.

"Oh, you can laugh, you have Mary to..."

"To cool my soup? You'd be married too, only you couldn't find a dowry big enough. Now pay from them drinks and stop your maudling!"

Hannah greeted her daughter's return to the car with a scowl.

"You said you wouldn't be long."

"It wasn't my fault, there was a huge queue!" Elaine handed over the cash and pension book.

"I don't know why you couldn't bring me this evening... at my usual time. You know as well as I do how busy the mornings are!" Hannah counted the cash carefully before consigning it to her purse. "And the supermarket will be just as bad, all those old fogies crawling around the place..."

Old fogies, Elaine thought, *and you pushing eighty yourself.*

"You could stay in the car, Mother, there's no need..."

"No need, you say? No need? Isn't it bad enough that I'm housebound all week, without locking me in the car when I get my only chance to do my bit of shopping?"

"Nobody is locking you anywhere. You go across to the centre nearly every day, you go to bingo twice a week and you go to the pub with *the holy water hens* every Saturday after Mass..." She pulled into a wheelchair bay beside the supermarket's main entrance.

"Go on, like a good girl, and get me a trolley. Collect me in the coffee shop in about an hour."

An hour? Shit! Elaine thought, watching her mother wheel her trolley through the entrance. Lighting a cigarette, she activated her mobile phone.

Mick Nevin clamped his hands – right over left – on the knob of his blackthorn stick, its shaft warping beneath his leaning weight. From behind and above came the excited bleating of lambs, revelling in their first experience of the freedom of the mountain. The ewes were calling too, their tones betraying the concern born of previous visits to the high pasture, a world away from the *crèche*-like security of the home paddock. A blue collie emerged, tongue lolling, from a clump of blooming gorse, and flopped wearily at its master's feet.

"I know, boy, I know. I'm feeling it too. We're getting too old for this lark but what are we to do? Lie down and die like Dan Murty beyond? Wouldn't he gladly swap places with us today? But no, he had to up and sell. Well, he didn't enjoy much of his money below in the town. I doubt he spent a month's interest..." The collie yawned, making a squeaking sound, and stretched to lie prone on his right flank. "Not one month's interest." Taking his right hand from the stick, Mick crouched and ruffled the thick scruff around the back of the sheepdog's neck. "Not one month's interest, I'd wager! What do you say to that, Bogey, what do you say to that, hah?"

Once the evening roast was in the oven and Hannah happily *tut-tutting* over the court reports in the local paper, Elaine took her keys from her bag and started towards the door.

"How long will you be?" Hannah demanded without removing her eyes from the account of a neighbour's drink-driving case.

"I'll be back by four... at the latest."

"I hope so. The child will be expecting her dinner." The door slammed.

Child indeed! Elaine grimaced. Her daughter was almost nineteen and studying to repeat her Leaving Cert in a final attempt to gain enough points to join her brother at the university in Cork.

I'd better be finished by then, an ironic gleam brightened Elaine's eye, *Sarah isn't the only one who'll be coming home at four...*

Across the river, Mick Nevin monitored the progress of the white Toyota Corolla from his doorstep. He sighed, shaking his head as the car swung left into the tarmac driveway of a pristine dormer bungalow.

"There's no justice, Bogey!" The collie looked up enquiringly at the sound of his name. "No justice at all." Mick checked his watch and whistled softly. "I thought 'twas a bit late all right; we'll have to keep an eye out." He chuckled dryly, "This could be a close one. Yes, sir, this could be a very close one. Come on, Bogey, we'll have time for a mouthful of tea anyway."

It was a close one but not close enough for Mick's liking. The white Corolla had just cleared the driveway when a black Golf appeared on the brow of the bridge.

"There's no justice, Bogey!" Mick swirled the remaining tea and leaves around in his mug before emptying them on the ash heap in the corner of the haggard.

The dog chose to ignore the words in favour of licking the final morsels of food from his enamel bowl.

"That's right, you're as bad as the rest of them: why should you worry as long as your own needs are satisfied? There's no justice, Bogey, no justice at all!" The dog eyed his master for a moment before stretching to nuzzle Mick's arthritically mis-shapen fingers. "You're a good boy, Bogey, where would I be without you?"

Hannah plonked her teacup on her empty dinner plate. "It'll be on the Thursday next week." She muttered.

"What will?" Elaine rose from the table and began to gather the used cutlery.

"Pension day! They're paying us on Thursday... because of Good Friday. And don't you try to tell me that you won't be able to take me in the afternoon... not after all the torture that you've put me through today."

"Torture, my eye. Look, I'll do the best I can but I'll have to change a few things around." Elaine's reward was a dubious *humph* from her mother.

Good Friday! Easter, how did I forget? Elaine agonised, running the hot water tap. Even the slightest disruption to Elaine's schedule had consequences. Single bank holidays were awkward enough, but Easter was as bad as Christmas – maybe worse, without any of the yuletide distractions and with all the problems that resulted from an extended school closure... and no night classes either. Good Fridays were a total disaster: no pubs, no bingo, even the bloody choir practice would be cancelled!

Mick knew the timetable as well as any man in the parish. He hadn't missed a visitation on his side of the bridge for almost five years. It was the change of car that had fooled him then: after three years of watching for a red Fiesta, he could be forgiven for not noticing the white Corolla.

Other than the ticking of the ancient eight-day clock, the only sound in the kitchen was the occasional clinking scrape of Mick's dinner plate, propelled across the flagged floor by the sheepdog's eager tongue.

"There's no justice, Bogey; no justice at all." The clock chimed seven times. Mick removed his grimy cap and got stiffly to his feet. He had plenty of time for a bath before cadging a lift into town on the bingo bus.

"Mum?" Rachel hovered uncertainly in the kitchen doorway.

"How much?" Elaine asked resignedly.

"Please, Mum, I need a hundred..." Elaine drew her daughter into the kitchen, pulling the door shut behind her.

"A *hundred*? What do you need a hundred for?"

"The girls are going to Cork for the weekend, to check out possible accommodation for college. They have a place to stay and... and... they've invited me along." She shrugged pleadingly. Elaine wasn't quite convinced.

"Girls... what girls... who...?"

"Judy Russell, Emma Cunningham and Sharon Joyce. Sharon's mother is our science teacher; she's driving us down and collecting us again on Sunday evening. Come on, Mum, you know them all." Elaine knew who they were all right, but she was no longer listening. The names had seared through her flesh like lead-weighted treble-hooks, the barbs now lodged deep within her gut. She reached for her purse and withdrew three crinkled fifty-euro notes.

"Nothing strange?" Matt asked, when Mick joined him at the bar counter.

"I let the lambs off today; I'd say we're over the worst of the weather."

"It must have been lovely up there today; any sign of a swallow yet?"

"Ah, 'twill be a few more weeks. Tell me this, Matt, do you miss it, the land I mean; were you ever sorry for bailing out?" Matt seemed to digest the question for a moment before replying.

"On days like today, maybe... but if you ever hear me saying that I miss the meadow or the bog or pulling *buachaláns* or scouring drains, sign me into the mad house straight away! I suppose you heard that Din Joe took a turn?"

"A pity 'twasn't the brother!" He paid for the drinks. "Jojo had a close one today, she was late arriving and was barely out the gate when the wife came home from school."

"There's still no guarantee that you'd get Jojo's place."

"But I wouldn't have to be watching week-after-week."

"You shouldn't be watching *any* week. Down on your knees you should be, with your Rosary beads, praying for a happy death!" Both bodies shook with mirth.

"Sure isn't there a bed ready above for me for years. Doesn't The Almighty well know that I haven't had an occasion of sin since the shillings and pence went out?"

It was on the following Monday morning that Mick's phone rang. Directly after the call, he drove his Range Rover into town and parked beside the bank. Four times he punched his PIN into the ATM before slipping a wad of crisp fifty-euro notes into his wallet. His next call was the drapers, from where he ferried an assortment of large carrier bags back to the jeep before returning home. Less than an hour later, the activity within the stone farmhouse had become too much for Bogey to endure. With a half-hearted snarl, he tucked his feathery tail between his legs and withdrew to a shady spot beneath the holly tree in the haggard.

By Friday morning, Mick had conceded that the crowd below the bridge mightn't be that bad after all. George the Major, Sonny Connor, Jack Cunningham and Curly Russell were all good neighbours and even Jojo Joyce had his good points, despite not appreciating his luck in being married to a teacher.

The white Corolla finally arrived just after four o'clock. A moment after her soft curves had darkened the doorway, Elaine's blonde hair brushed Mick's cheek.

"I hope you've had that bath, Mick, first impressions matter!" She whispered, undoing the buttons of her black lace blouse.

BEYOND LIMBO

Madge awoke with a start and raised the duvet to shield her eyes against the low shaft of morning sunlight that glared through her window. Sighing, she dropped her head back onto the pillow and listened. All was quiet. *Good,* she thought, a little quiver of anticipation surging within. There and then she resolved to make the most of every moment before...

September was such a beautiful month. Even as a school-child, Madge had understood precisely what had moved to poet to write of *'season of mists and mellow fruitfulness'*. Early autumn had a certain, gentle, almost apologetic quality, as though compensating in advance for the harsher months ahead. Jack would have the turf home by now; the long hours of backbreaking toil that had devoured a summer of evenings and Saturdays had finally borne fruit...

But Jack had retired... She could see him now, lifting the round ripe onions from their withering roots and then laying them to save on the sun-caked bed from whence they had sprung. Jack adored gardening; it was as if each carefully nurtured plant was another small compensation for the new life that their union had deserved. Madge also loved the garden, but not just for the bounty it provided for the table. To her, the garden meant so much more: buzzing bees, fluttering butterflies, little daring robins, dust-bathing sparrows, colourful tits and finches and, best of all, the throaty symphonies of territorial blackbirds, late into the lengthening spring evenings. Of all the things she missed since losing her independence, blackbird song was the greatest loss of all...

Nobody had given them a chance back then: eighteen-year-old Madge, innocent of the ways of the world and Jack, an apparently confirmed bachelor, much closer to the half-century than the quarter. But Jack had shown her a new kind of love and, in time, she too learned to return that most precious of blessings. If the expression, *'without an idle bone in his body',* ever applied to anyone, then it most certainly would have applied to Jack. Despite his early morning starts and long hours of stone cutting in the quarry, his desire for her happiness was insatiable. Madge would only have to make a passing comment on some aspect of a neighbour's house and Jack would immediately set about making the relevant alterations to their own home...

The unmistakable jingle of metal on crockery heralded the approach of the breakfast trolley, but it was still too far away to hazard a guess at the attendant's identity. Would it be the young red-haired girl who always had a kind word or would it be the hatchet-faced older lady whose heartlessness may simply be the result of too many years in the job? Or perhaps it might be the friendly foreign man with the permanent delay in his deformed leg, which he dragged uncomplainingly behind him.

Madge often wondered if his handicap was the result of political conflict in his native land or whether his misfortune was due to some cruel genetic quirk or even the primitive birthing procedures of an underdeveloped country. So many times she had wanted to ask him but, even if she could have managed to make herself heard, there would still have been his difficulty with the language... Yet, despite this communication problem, he still understood her far better than most.

On days like today, when she had no desire to eat, he would discreetly clear the food from her plate, tear it into tiny fragments and slip it through the open window for the squabbling beaks that waited below. She tried to think of his name. Was it *Ken*-something? Not Kenneth... no, it was something else... He reminded her of Jack on a Sunday morning: with that bittersweet aroma of stale porter and half-smoked cigarettes. No, it wasn't *Ken*; it was *Kim*... something or, maybe *Kem*... That was it; Kemal was the man's name. Kemal was the father of six children; Jack had been the father of one, but only for a few short hours... John and Patrick, his grandfathers' names, were what Madge had decided to christen their son, just minutes before the midwife broke the terrible news...

John Patrick would have been the same age as Mrs. Wilson's boy. For over eighteen years, she had watched Harry grow and each and every time she looked at the sprouting lad, she had fought the urge to wonder... what if... what if? It had somehow become even worse after Harry had left home... it was then that she and Mrs. Wilson had become almost friends. It was as if Mrs. Wilson's loss – a sort of little death – had brought the neighbours temporarily closer, until his mother's joy at each visit from Harry forced a wedge of jealousy back between them. When Madge would eventually find the strength to stop for another chat, Mrs. Wilson would remind her of how lucky she was to have Jack, compared to waking each morning to an empty silent house.

Mrs. Wilson was dead now... three years... or was that Jack? No Jack had gone to his reward a long time before that... Madge had wanted to die then too but suicide was a mortal sin and mortal sin barred access to Heaven... The Wilsons were Church of Ireland. Did Protestants go to Heaven? Would she meet with Mrs. Wilson again... if only for the tiniest fragment of eternity... two strutting young mothers, comparing notes on the progress of their healthy baby boys? Would Captain Wilson be there? She could see him quite clearly now: a dashing dark moustachioed figure in his fighter-pilot's uniform, a proud father going off to fight and die for a better world for his infant son and for all children everywhere. Perhaps, this time around, Jack would forgive his neighbour for enlisting with the old enemy... they might even go for a celestial pint together...

But, if republican Catholics and British soldiers went to the same Heaven, would there be Germans there too? And Jews... and Americans and maybe even some Japanese? And what about Muslims, or did they just go to purgatory along with the other pagans, or was that the other place? She would ask... what's his name? He was quite dark skinned, he might know... if she could only think of his name... Jack would know... she would ask Jack just as soon as he came home...

The trolley was closer now. Madge could hear the rippling of pouring tea but the absence of both friendly banter and the squeaks of a rubber sole being dragged across polished floor tiles did not bode well. Madge closed her eyes and feigned sleep; perhaps the awful creature might just let her be. She felt the food tray being jammed into position but kept her face buried in the pillow. Rough fingers bit into the translucent skin of her good arm and began to rock her violently. Inwardly screaming, Madge opened her eyes and, mouth clamped tightly shut, shook her head pleadingly.

"Come on now, *Maggie*, I haven't got time for your tantrums today. I've got other people to look after. Come on, up!" Madge found herself being jerked upright and, in an effort to avoid further pain, attempted to comply but her body refused to respond. She could feel the snarl of thin lips against her temple as the hissed words exploded in her eardrum.

"Get up, you old hag or I'll...!" Magde felt her arm drop limply back against the comfort of the duvet.

I did try, I really did try! She wanted to say but, despite the fact that no sound would come, it appeared that her tormentor had got the message.

"Very well, *Maggie*, have it your way!" The hissing had mellowed to her more accustomed sneer but the voice sounded as though it came from a great distance, the words continued to flow but from farther and farther away... "We'll see what Matron has to say..."

Plans for Madge's future were well advanced. Her parents were on the brink of finalizing a match with a young farmer from the neighbouring parish. Teddy was a good-looking lad, tall and athletic, just a few years her senior. Madge's mother swore by him: an only son with nearly fifty acres of arable land, plus access to a few hundred more of mountain commonage. Her dowry was in place and her father had arranged to walk Teddy's land on Whit Sunday... and then Madge discovered the rambling house...

It was ironic that it should have been Nora, Teddy's sister, who had suggested the evening out. Neither of Madge's parents had been musically inclined and their old wet-and-dry battery radio had been strictly reserved for news bulletins and weather forecasts...

It was the familiar thump-squeak-flop that forced Madge back to consciousness. But why was he coming now? Had she not eaten breakfast already? There was no way she could stomach another morsel... even for... *Ken* or *Al* or whatever the nice dark gentleman was called. His distinctive odours came wafting through to her now, she could sense him bending over her... but the voice she heard was not his. The accent was cultured, educated but definitely Irish... just like... like... am... what was the name of the young Protestant boy who lived in the big house at the end of their avenue? Had she dreamt it or had Mrs. Wilson mentioned something about Harry studying medicine? She raised her head and soon two white-coated figures began to swim in and out of focus...

The scene in Murphy's cottage on that summer night would be forever imprinted on Madge's brain. Nora had led the way, opening the backdoor as if she had lived there all of her life. As one, a sea of heads turned to view the new arrivals. Many nodded, a few hands waved but nobody spoke until the little druid of a man who stood before the open hearth had finished his song. As the applause died, there was a shuffling of feet as bodies pushed closer together in an effort to make room for the girls. In a moment, a space appeared on the edge of the green homemade furm that stretched along the whitewashed wall from their entry point to the door that led to one of two bedrooms behind the chimneystack.

Once seated, Nora introduced her prospective sister-in-law to a blur of strangers. Most were servant boys and girls, many of whom had abandoned their distant homes to seek employment in the more fertile inland parts of the county. From fresh-faced youngsters to seasoned veterans, all were armed with the songs, steps and tunes of their own townlands. United by their isolation, new friendships would blossom between recent strangers until the completion of the harvest would see their temporary community fracture and scatter with the autumn leaves...

Her arm was being lifted again, but tenderly now... She turned her head slightly and noted how the scars on Kemal's hands bore testimony to years of toil. How old would he be? It was hard to tell, but the signature of hardship was etched beneath his deep dark eyes and the widening streaks of grey that brightened his thick wavy hair. The cultured voice sounded again.

"I'm reconnecting your drip and don't remove it again!" She felt the burning prick of the hollow needle being inserted into the bruised vein on the back of her right hand. She squeezed her eyes against a well of tears and, when her vision cleared, stared into the unrecognising gaze of Harry Wilson.

It's me, her brain screamed. *It's me, Madge... Madge Breen. You must remember me... you have to!* But he had already turned away...

As the magic evening progressed, amid much gaiety and an occasional tear, the performances continued to flow with haphazard efficiency. To Madge, time seemed to stand still. Enthralled, she ogled each intricate step of the swirling dancers and absorbed the joy and pain of every song or recitation but it was the sound of the fiddle that touched her most deeply of all. Though the fiddler was neither tall nor broad, he had the biggest hands she had ever seen. His fingers fascinated her, they were not long and artistic like those of the church organist; they were simply huge in every way, like a bunch of off-colour bananas. Bewitched, she listened and stared, hearing and seeing, but not quite believing how such ungainly looking objects could have such amazing dexterity... Somehow, she felt that she knew him, but there was something amiss... It was like fitting all the pieces of a jigsaw puzzle together and ending up with a picture that didn't make any sense...

There was a new sound now, a harsh rasping sound and everything became suddenly darker. Somebody was drawing the screens around her bed, perhaps young Dr. Harry was returning... but there was a new scent... a pungent cocktail of aftershave lotion, carbolic soap and brandy. The priest! How long since he had last visited her... she remembered now, it was over a year ago, just after she had suffered the stroke. She could have laughed out loud at his obvious disappointment when he had realised that she was no longer able to reach her purse. *Ah well,* she had reasoned, *no tenner, no visit!* At least she knew how things stood.

Absently, she wondered where her rosary beads were and then remembered: she had given them to Kemal during his wife's difficult pregnancy. It hadn't occurred to her then but now she smiled at the thought of a devout Muslim arriving home with a rosary beads that had been blessed at the sacred grotto of Lourdes. The priest was mumbling inaudibly; something cold and sticky touched her brow: baby-soft fingers… This was it; he was preparing her for the journey…

Nora was clearly bothered when she returned from dancing the *Siege of Ennis*. Red-faced and breathless, she began her confession to Madge. Her real reason for wanting to come to the rambling house had been to meet with a young man that she'd had her eye on for some time. Tonight it had happened, he had offered her a lift home on the bar of his bicycle and, in her eagerness to accept, she had forgotten about Madge. Then came the softly spoken words from beneath the stairs.

"I'm going your way, I'd be glad to walk with you to your boreen… if you'd like." Madge turned and found herself face to face with the fiddler. Anticipating defeat, he started towards the door and, fitting his cap, made Madge's picture complete.

She did know him, she'd known him all of her life. If it was safe to walk the road with anyone, that person had to be Jack Breen. As good as his word, Jack wheeled his bicycle every step of the way, patiently answering her eager questions, explaining the difference between jigs and reels, polkas and slides, and eventually agreeing to guide her through the *Walls of Limerick* at the next gathering. The first birds were beginning to chirp as Madge skipped her way along the cart-rutted track, towards the candle that still burned in the window of the squat farmhouse. More songsters were roused into retaliation but the waking notes of their dawn chorus were wasted on the excited girl, her ears were still ringing to the enchanting tones of Jack Breen's fiddle…

Madge sensed movement as the curtain parted slightly and there was a gentle thud to her right. She opened her eyes to see Kemal staring back at her in disbelief, his eyes reflecting the light of the candle he had just placed on her bedside locker.

"You better again, I get doctor?" He looked as if had seen a ghost.

That's what I am, she thought, *I'm a ghost, floating between two dimensions!* Mustering her strength, she shook her head as vigorously as she was able. Kemal got the message.

"No doctor? Some other thing, tea... water?" She nodded and tried to smile...

If Madge's parents had been disappointed by her refusal to go through with the match, they were totally devastated when she announced that she was walking out with Jack Breen. If only they had accepted the situation, the relationship might have run its course and died a natural death but, the more they opposed her; the more she rebelled. They had made it very plain: there would be no dowry for any daughter of theirs who would marry a man without land. Until that announcement, the thought of marriage to Jack Breen had never crossed Madge's mind...

Madge was sitting upright when Kemal returned with the water. Briefly, her fingers brushed his muscular forearm as he placed a glass beside the candle. Nodding her thanks, she managed a tight smile. He waved and disappeared through the curtain. As his irregular footfalls faded, she gripped the tube of the drip between her gums and forced her hand forward until the needle slipped from the vein. Her hand now free of the restriction, she reached inside the locker and felt for the case of her rosary beads. Forcing back the spring-loaded lid, she emptied the contents onto the duvet.

Well before her stroke, she had told them that she didn't need sleeping tablets, but they just wouldn't listen. She selected one now, palmed it into the functioning side of her mouth, took a sip of water and swallowed. As she continued to repeat the process, she reasoned that, if there really was a god, of whatever colour or creed, how could he – or she – deny any soul the chance to finally soar beyond limbo?

UNCLE JOHNSEY

It's funny but I'd never noticed it before. Funny, in the sense that I'd only noticed it now was because it wasn't there. Oh, the gateway was there, but overgrown, not cropped in readiness for Dad to park his car on the paved passage. Well, he wasn't my real dad: I'd got him when I was about ten... Before that, Mum and I would travel on the ferry from Liverpool, then by train to the town where Uncle Johnsey would meet us and drive us to Gran's in his blue VW Beetle.

From my very first visit, the view from the summit of the hill above the village had sent my heart racing. The long hours spent on ferry and trains were all suddenly worthwhile. The dazzlingly whitewashed homestead was in sharp contrast with the greens, browns and golds of the land, the surf-maned turquoise of the bay and the brooding indigo of the mountains on the opposite peninsula.

"The crooked wall at the hairpin bend, west of the house, is our boundary with Denny Collins and the passage down to the shore bounds us on this side!" The pride in Johnsey's voice was infectious. Just a couple of generations back, his ancestors had killed and died for these very stony fields. *Our boundary,* Johnsey had said, and from that moment I'd felt part of it too.

Later, when my baby brother arrived, I'd feared that the presence of a male child in the family might undermine my relationship with Johnsey but I needn't have worried. From the beginning, Johnsey had made me feel special and, even after my second brother had been born, nothing changed. Each year, Johnsey continued to equip me with a new pair of red wellies, to wear on our bird watching and fishing expeditions or when collecting driftwood and shells along the foreshore.

Warm dusty August, with her seasoned grasses wilting beneath bursts of flaming fuscia, montbretia and rambling nasturtium; snow-freckled from Johnsey's annual whitewashing of house, piers and walls in celebration of the emigrants' return.

Now, spreading blotches of moss and lichen bore testament to the protracted absence of brush and lime from the weathered stone. The flora too was unfamiliar, the roadside verges were now clad in cooler hues: ranks of wilting daffodil divided fragrant blizzards of blackthorn from sprinkles of timid bluebell and aromatic primrose.

Heavy and unmoved by the joys of spring, my heart was pining for the wonders of Augusts past and childhood outgrown. Sighing, I hitched up my long dress and, after struggling over the stone stile beside the gate pier, picked my steps past the turf shed at the leeward gable.

It wasn't a shed by today's standards, more of a lean-to really: a roof of rusting corrugated iron, supported by four discarded telephone poles, which Granda had erected before Mum had been born. I'd never seen it empty before; Johnsey had always taken pride in having the fuel saved and home before the first meadow would fall to the mowing bar.

Though Mum would always bring a carton of duty-free cigarettes, I'd never seen her smoke in Gran's presence. Her secret supply would be hidden at the back of Johnsey's first aid locker in the dairy, to be visited whenever Gran took a snooze or the tension between mother and daughter became too much to bear. Once, when we were about nine, Marie Collins and I raided Mum's stash and we were just about to light up when Johnsey appeared from nowhere and caught us in the act.

"Put them back and clear off!" He'd snapped. *"If I ever catch you again..."* He never did. I lit a cigarette now and, after a furtive glance around, ducked my head beneath the low lintel at the stall entrance. Momentarily startled by some creature scurrying along the slurry channel, I blinked to adjust my eyes to the dim interior. It was darker than I remembered but I soon realised that this was due to the thick layers of dust-laden cobwebs that clouded the few sheets of Perspex that had been built into the iron roof. One-by-one, I lifted the cows' tie-ropes, remembering the names of the docile individuals who had stood, patiently chewing their cud, while Johnsey's calloused fingers coaxed the rich bounty from their swollen udders. I could al-

most hear the rhythmic *pess-pesh, pess-pesh* of the twin needle-thin jets, squirting into the frothing bucket below.

There had been other sounds too: deep stomach rumbles, cloven hooves scraping against cobblestones and the occasional stifled oath from Johnsey when a beast would chose the most inopportune of moments to relieve herself. Smells wafted back through the decades, that uniquely bovine cocktail of steam, urine and faeces, tempered with disinfectant and carbolic soap from Johnsey's teat-washing cloths. I could picture them now, their sleek sloping backs in an undulating row: the reds, roans, blues and greys of their British Shorthorn breed. Sighing, I returned to the present and the daylight, under the dark feral eyes of a skittish semi-circle of pale Charalois bullocks.

I found my gaze drawn sideways to the dung-heap at the rear of the byre. Long free of the persistent scratching of poultry, the decaying mound had been colonised by a profusion of perennial weeds... What a change from the days when, just as soon as the last haycock had been crowned, Johnsey would tackle the donkey and draw the manure to stimulate the meadows into one last burst of growth, that would feed the livestock until housing time.

Straying from the cobbled passage, my stiletto heels began to sink as I approached the hayshed: my all-embracing bolthole from unpleasant chores, feuding adults and sudden summer showers. Though empty, except for a solitary foraging robin, it was more full of memories than ever.

There is something about August rain that can drive people mad. For some, it's the obvious threat to the harvest; for others, the frustration of dampened holiday plans and unfulfilled hopes. For us, those determined drizzles foreshadowed the inevitable tears when visiting relatives would depart, leaving old sores to remain unsalved.

I had loved the odd rainy day and had liked nothing better than to snuggle into a cosy hollow in the butt of the previous year's fodder and listen to a thundershower batter and spatter against the high arched roof. I took a final drag before discarding my cigarette and allowed my thoughts to wander yet again.

The cats were invariably the first farmyard refugees to seek the protection of the hayshed. Their approach was always cautious, making little darting runs, then pausing, suspecting danger around every corner. I would watch the cats, their heads oscillating as parent swallows swooped to dive-bomb all intruders. Gradually the birds would relax and resume the feeding of their nestlings, high up in the iron girders that supported the roof. The cats would soon settle and, except for an occasional upward glance, concentrate on meticulously grooming their colourful coats.

Next would come the hens with their strutting rooster, a handful of precocious bantams and the few turkey chicks, hatched by a broody hen, specifically for the Christmas table. The poultry benefited on the double from the shed, not only did they gain shelter from the elements but they had the additional bonus of a veritable feast from the various invertebrates they managed to unearth from beneath the musty hay.

Charlie would always be the last to join our menagerie. While the black-and-white collie was much valued as a willing and effective cattle dog, he really saw his role as that of guardian, not only of the household but also of the roadway outside. His chosen sentry post was between the piers of the rarely used wicket-gate at the front of the dwelling house. It took more than a few drops of rain to deter Charlie from seeing off any vehicle that dared to encroach on his territory. He would be already saturated even before the gushing torrents from the gutter-less roof gave him a final drenching. Once inside the shed, his first action would be to shake himself vigorously. As chickens squawked their protests, cats would dash for cover, sometimes retreating too far and ending up back out in the rain again.

Oblivious to the consternation his arrival had caused, Charlie would nuzzle up to me, lay his head on my lap and promptly fall asleep. Soon the steam would begin to rise from his drying coat and the smell of wet dog would hang in the heavy air. From the moment I'd first met Charlie, I had wanted a dog of my own.

"We can't keep a dog in a flat", Mum would say, *"if we had a house…"* Harry had a house. I called him *Dad* earlier, but his

name is Harry. Harry had a great house and, when Mum and I went to live with him, it was like entering a different world. I had my very own room and there was a room for Mum too, but she usually slept with either Harry or me. Harry's house had two gardens: the little one in front was full of flowers, but the back one was huge and had lots of room for a dog. I pointed this out to Mum but she said that we couldn't get a dog until after the baby came...

Even by the standards of the time, Johnsey's farming methods would have been considered old-fashioned. His hayshed would stand empty for several weeks after the tardiest of his neighbours had completed the harvest.

"It's the swallows," he'd argue, "If the hay was in now, sure the cats would be able to reach the nests!" But Johnsey's harvest also began after everyone else's.

"How could I cut any earlier? Aren't corncrakes scarce enough without me chopping them up with the mower?" Had been his perennial response to Gran's nagging.

Even though I'd never been there to see the conclusion of the hay season, I'd always played my part in the saving. At first, my job had been to ferry tea and sandwiches to Johnsey in the meadow but, as I got older, my duties became more technical. By the age of six, I was a dab hand at standing on the haycocks and stamping each new forkful into position on the growing mounds. Within a few years, I could turn, toss and rake with the best of my local contemporaries.

It was in the meadow that I'd finally discovered Charlie's secret. Though I'd never been awake for the morning milking, Charlie's evening punctuality had never ceased to amaze me. Regardless of the weather or whatever the current farm task happened to be, Charlie would set off to bring the cows in for milking at six o'clock precisely. I had posed the question to each adult in turn: I firmly believe that neither Mum nor Gran actually knew the answer, but Johnsey was a different matter.

"Dogs sometimes know things that we don't." He would repeat and then ruffle the dog's scruff. "Isn't that right, Charlie, isn't that right?"

It was one of those rare balmy evenings; even on the fore-shore there was hardly a puff of wind. We had just finished raking *Curlews' Meadow* and, while Johnsey swallowed a mug of water, I listened to the faint serenading of an amorous bull from somewhere across the bay. Suddenly, Charlie sprang from apparent sleep into instant action and, hurdling the open dou-ble-ditch between the meadows, headed for the pasture. I sup-pose, I'd only heard it because my ears had already been tuned into the bull but there it was, a very faint peal. I waited a few moments and heard another, with two more in quick succes-sion, then a pause and then another... Johnsey was studying me closely, a twinkle in his grey eyes.

"You heard it, didn't you?" Yes, I'd heard it all right, the six o'clock Angelus bell from St. Matthew's Church in the vil-lage; the bell that tolled and told Charlie to begin the evening roundup. Yes, dogs do know some things that we don't and, to this day, I'm grateful to Johnsey for allowing me to solve that particular little mystery by myself.

I checked my watch; I still had nearly an hour before... I was facing the rear of the dwelling house now or, more correctly, the flat roofed extension that Johnsey had added to the original structure, shortly after his father's death. To Gran, for whom indoor plumbing had been an impossible dream, the addition of a scullery with running water and an indoor flush toilet meant unimaginable luxury. It mattered little that water would still have to be heated on the peat-fuelled, black *Stanley* range, which stood in the recess of the kitchen's original open hearth.

My heart pounding, I tentatively reached my hand towards the ledge above the door, my fingers trembling as they closed on their target. The key was still there! I unlocked the door and slipped through to the kitchen. If the house had a soul, this would have been it. Occupying well over half of the ground floor area, it had a coped ceiling that extended all the way to the rafters that had supported the original thatched roof. The thatch had long since given way to slate but the dark cobwebbed hooks that clung to the high, blackened beams were a constant reminder of a more self-sufficient era. It was here that the home-salted bacon had hung to cure in the smoke of peat and wood, candle and pipe.

I think I was about three when we'd first visited Johnsey and Gran. Despite my youth, I could sense the tension between Mum and her mother. Johnsey was aware of it too, and always attempted to whisk me away at the first hint of trouble, but even he didn't get it right every time. The incident that sticks most in my mind happened after supper one night, at a time when it seemed that Mum and Gran were observing an uneasy truce.

The little farmhouse had only two bedrooms. These were accessed by the doors on either side of the chimneybreast and were occupied by Johnsey and Gran. Mum and I were billeted in the little attic space between their bedroom ceilings and the rafters. The only natural light source in the loft was a tiny gable window, which faced east and caught the very first glow of dawn above the darkness of the towering mountain. It was after I'd gone to bed that night that I gleaned further insight into the family dynamic. I'd discovered that, by placing myself beside the disused fireplace, I could easily keep tabs on the goings-on in the kitchen below.

Mum was teasing Johnsey again.

"So tell us, when are you going to find a woman for yourself?" I could picture his sheepish grin but it was Gran's voice that sounded.

"Not everybody is in the hurry that you were, madam!" I heard the scrape of chair legs on flagstone before the backdoor slammed.

"Now you've upset her again!" Johnsey sounded more defiant than usual.

"Hah!" Gran snorted. *"That's her lookout, we can all be touchy when it suits us! Wouldn't I look well if you brought some little trollop in under my roof? Isn't it enough that she got herself landed and, after all her smartness, was left to face the music alone?"*

"She is better off alone and single than married to..."

"And a lot you'd know about it!" Another chair scraped but this time it was a bedroom door that slammed. I promised my-

self right there and then that someday I would marry Johnsey and then everybody would live happily ever after. Moments later, the rich throaty warbles of a roosting blackbird banished the ominous silence and sleep released me from the painful world of grown-ups.

I had never been in Johnsey's bedroom, or Gran's either, that is until after she'd died and I'd helped Mum to sort out her stuff. I found myself turning the handle of Johnsey's door; it creaked slowly inward to reveal a iron-framed single bed, an open wardrobe, where a few items of working clothes dangled from wire hangers, and a little scattering of DIY tools, on top of a woodworm-riddled chest-of-drawers.

On impulse, I grabbed the Swiss Army Knife, the tool that had seemed so magical in Johnsey's hands. The tool that could do anything from peeling a windfall apple or paring the donkey's hooves, to lancing an abscess on a suffering beast or getting the Volkswagen moving again. Johnsey didn't need it now and, in spite of them all, I'd have something tangible to remember him by. I slipped the knife into my handbag and, after relocking the house, returned to my car.

It seemed that half of the county was gathering at St Matthew's church. Passing the pub, I could smell the food being prepared for afterwards...

"All fur coat and no knickers!" His big sister had said when she'd learned of Johnsey's interest in the widowed publican. Gran would never be dead while Mum lived! Do we all eventually become our mothers?

I watched the widow now, a shapely figure alighting from her designated car. Whatever about knickers, there was no fur coat, just a three-quarter-length navy dress with matching shoes and hat. I hastened my steps to assume my rightful place in the procession. Although I could never deliver on my promise to marry Johnsey, I was determined to make the most of being chief bridesmaid at his wedding.

HELL IN PARADISE

It was through a dusty port window of *The Adriatic Breeze*, the passenger ferry from Split to the island of Hvar, that Barry first saw her. Excitedly, he elbowed his companion's ribs.

"John, look. Look, the blonde!" Reluctantly, John looked up from his *Rough Guide to Croatia*.

"The blonde? They are *all* blonde!"

"Red baseball cap."

"With the tanned legs?"

"She is drop-dead-gorgeous!"

"How can a blonde get that tanned *before* a sun holiday?"

"Well, maybe like you, she spent a fortnight on a sun-bed." Barry breathed as the subject of their attention ascended the steps to board the catamaran.

"She's got brown eyes." John whispered as the girl removed her shades and sidestepped along the narrow aisle, past his seat.

"So?"

"I'll bet she isn't even a real blonde."

"As if it matters… but I would *love* to find out." Eyes closed, Barry conjured up the image.

"According to this, we're heading for *the islands of Hell*." John announced, closing his guide as the ferry approached Stari Grad pier.

"You can call them what you like but, right now, I'm looking *Heaven* straight in the face." John followed Barry's gaze to where his dream-girl shared a joke with a somewhat paler version of herself.

"They make a pretty pair all right." John conceded as he rose to take his place in the queue towards the exit.

"Yeah. Why don't you make a play for her friend and we'll all have a week to remember?"

"Hold on there, lover boy, we don't all hit on the first girl we see."

"Well, she is the most interesting sight that I've seen for a while." They joined the loose semi-circle of travellers that formed by the two waiting coaches at the pier-head. As the mound of transient luggage continued to change shape and colours, John grunted in satisfaction when an attendant in a white tee-shirt hoisted his trolley case into the hold of the nearer vehicle.

"Have you spotted your case?" He eyed Barry quizzically.

"Great, she's on our coach... look!"

"Has your case been loaded? It's not in that lot and I didn't notice it on the coach." John indicated the few items of luggage that remained on the sun-baked concrete.

"One minute." Barry did a quick check of both coaches as the luggage doors beeped shut. "It's not there, I'll bet the buggers left it on the ferry!" John gaped in astonishment as Barry sprinted past him and leapt from the pier onto the already revving boat. Moments later *The Adriatic Breeze* was making steady headway back towards the mainland.

From the left aisle-seat of the third row, a pair of dark eyes twinkled at John's increasing frustration with the disaffected coachman. The driver's face was a mask of controlled annoyance, clearly conditioned by many such encounters with excitable tourists. Despite the language barrier, there was no mistaking the driver's ultimatum. It made no difference to him whether John came aboard or remained at the pier, but one thing was certain: the coach was leaving and it was leaving now. With a final volley of protest, John brushed past the driver and flopped resignedly into the vacant seat across from the girl.

"He vill be ok, your friend?" John simply stared, words failing him. *Christ*, he thought, *Barry was right: she is gorgeous.*

"Oh him? He'd be all right now if he'd kept his mind on his luggage instead of... of..." He grinned sheepishly and offered his hand. "Sorry, my name is John and," he nodded in the general direction of the ocean, "in case we ever see him again, he's Barry."

"Yanna." The girl's grip was cool and brief; John shuddered as her hand swung to rest casually on her companion's forearm. "This is Helga, my great friend." Another solid handshake from another stunning girl; he almost felt sorry for Barry as he ogled the rebellious twin peaks that tested the delicate fabric of Yanna's white vest.

Great friend? John digested the term for a moment. *Surely it can't be...*he shook his head as if to rid his brain of the thought, *but if it is... what a waste... what a double waste.* His eyes lingered briefly on Helga's voluptuously parted lips. *I can't wait... but not yet... definitely, not just yet.*

At the Hvar bus station, the passengers disembarked to form tight little groups around their various tour representatives.

"It is an Irish flower on your friend's hat?" Yanna's fingers fluttered briefly above John's wristwatch.

"Flower? Oh, the shamrock? He insisted on wearing that thing; yes, we're Irish."

"Ve are from Germany," she volunteered, "so ve maybe see you on the island, yah? Ve stay at Paradiso in Vloka."

"We're at Meneghello." John was vaguely aware of the girls' continuing interest as he tried to communicate his concerns about Barry's absence to a series of disinterested couriers.

"There is many ferry to Palmizana. He come soon; you see," was all the satisfaction he could draw from one pair of heavily glossed lips.

"But it wouldn't have happened if your people did their job properly."

"Please, is too hot for this argue. There is many ferry..."

"I know, I know. *He come soon... you see.*" Jerking his suitcase aloft, he joined the dozen-or-so occupants of the little cabin cruiser destined for Palmizana on the island of Sveti Kliment.

The cooling breeze on the open-decked boat instantly changed John's perspective for the better. Gone was the stifling claustrophobic sensation of the coach trip through the arid mountain trail from Stari Grad to the town of Hvar. Now the translucent waters of the Adriatic lapped soothingly below the gunwales of the purring craft, while ahead, the soft outline of the little verdant island seemed to nestle snugly against an endless sweep of unadulterated azure sky. He allowed his thoughts to drift with his eyes, only vaguely aware of the little snippets of conversation that intruded from his fellow passengers. It sounded as though Ireland was well represented: a Dublin 4 tone waxed lyrically on the merits of the new series BMW, a couple of female voices discussed the more pressing issue of sun-block factors, while the efforts of some unseen Germans and Dutch to discuss the European Soccer Finals were drowned by a heated provincial debate on the Munster Hurling Championship.

With Cork clinging to a precarious lead, the Palmizana marina swung into view. Once the human cargo had been disgorged from the vessel, a couple of bronzed bare-chested youths conveyed the luggage to a battered yellow jeep before directing their visitors up the steep track towards the restaurant and its guest accommodation. As John fell into step at the rear of the little posse, the mingled aromas of lavender and rosemary instantly replaced the dissipating diesel fumes from the growling vehicle. From somewhere high up on an almost naked fir tree, came the whirring staccato clicks of cicada song, while, to the right of the track, an incandescent green-brown lizard scurried towards the safety of the crisp undergrowth.

Once inside his *en-suite* room, the effects of travel fatigue took instant priority over John's initial concerns about having to share a bed with another man. The tranquillising aural cocktail from the incessant cicadas and the cooling hum of his ceiling fan soon provided an irresistible lullaby to a body deprived of sleep for over thirty hours. After what seemed like a few fleeting moments, John's slumber was unceremoniously desecrated by a persistent hammering sound. Unlocking the door, John blinked as Barry stormed past him to flop wearily onto the dishevelled bed.

"So much for your research; nobody has a bloody word of English." Barry groaned, sweat streaming from his flushed brow.

"At least you got your luggage back!"

"Yeah, after five hours of chasing people around bloody Split."

"*Split?*" John's eyes swung questioningly from his watch back to the red-faced speaker.

"Yeah, Split. My luggage was never on the bloody ferry in the first place. You've no idea what I've been through. They wanted to charge me for the return trip... *again*! I'll never..." John had heard enough.

"Her name is Yanna." His catalogue of disasters forgotten, Barry's blue eyes sparkled.

"You spoke to her?"

"And Helga, they're on the island too."

"Our island, where?" Barry pulled off his saturated shirt. "I'm taking a shower; then we've got hunting to do."

About thirty minutes later, John sighed and reluctantly forced his eyes from the black-and-white ballet of a pair of Hungarian Glider butterflies.

"What is it now?"

"There isn't even a road to the place!" Barry whinged, pointing to the narrow rocky path that extended beyond the signpost that declared: *Vloka 1.5km.* "Besides, that sign says nothing about Paradiso." He added dejectedly.

"Paradiso is a restaurant in Vloka, and, talking about restaurants, I could do with some food right now; it seems a long time since that snack on the plane." John started down the gravelled path, lined by towering red and yellow cactus flowers, towards the enticing aroma of barbecuing lamb. As soon as they were seated in the Meneghello restaurant, Barry whistled softly.

"Hey, look at those two over there."

"What about them?" John asked without removing his eyes from the intriguing menu.

"Oh, shit!" Barry hissed.

"What now?"

"They're holding hands." This time John did look as the girls self-consciously disengaged to light cigarettes.

"So? Live and let live."

"Yeah, you're right; I mean what man would fancy either of that pair anyway?"

"Look, I don't know if you've noticed, but we've only got one double bed; I'd better talk to someone about it." The words brought an unexpected grin to Barry's scorched features.

87

"If we have a double bed, the chances are that the girls have the same situation..."

"But, those girls..."

"No buts, just follow my lead and you can call when we toss to decide which couple stays where."

Following Barry's lead proved to be more onerous than John had reckoned with. Just after six o'clock, Barry donned his shorts and walking boots and browbeat his reluctant cohort into accompanying him along the uneven woodland path towards the girls' location. Despite the intensity of the sun and the demands of the extra hours of travel, Barry's white legs pumped determinedly towards his goal, pausing only once to ask a question of John.

"What's making all that clicking racket in those trees?"

"*Cvrci...* cicadas to you."

"And the same to you, but what's making all the noise?"

"They are actually members of the locust family."

"Don't they ever take a break?"

"You'd be making a racket too if you had spent seventeen years underground."

"Ah. So, it's a mating call?"

"I thought you might empathise with that." Grinning broadly, Barry had another question.

"And I suppose they die afterwards?" John tilted his water bottle, nodding as he swallowed. "And I suppose there's some kind of a moral in that too?" John's reply was a silent shrug, before resuming his journey with an amused grin.

After almost thirty minutes of steady walking, the faint strains of civilization began to filter through the lush foliage of the pine forest. Moments later, the thirsty pair clinked half-litre tumblers together before taking lusty swallows of ice-cold Croatian lager.

"Paradiso." Barry gulped, his eyes fruitlessly scanning the assembled diners. "It's still early." He muttered, as though to reaffirm the validity of their mission to himself.

"Paradiso." John echoed. "This beer isn't too bad."

"Shit!"

"What's wrong with it?"

"Not the beer; look at the menu!"

"But, we've just eaten!"

"You said Paradiso was a restaurant; this menu says *Dionis!*"

"Shit!" Finishing the beer took seconds; the uphill jog to Paradiso took five minutes.

Spotting the red baseball cap, Barry was instantly inspired into action.

"They're at the corner table. Go on over, they know you; I'll bring the drinks." John nodded compliantly; the evening might provide some entertainment after all. Experiencing a sudden surge of anticipation, John detoured by the toilet to compose his thoughts. Pausing at the washbasin, he dampened his fingers to comb his thick dark hair back from his tanned forehead... *just in case*... Dessert was served as he reached the girls' table; Yanna's welcome seemed genuinely warm.

"It is John, yah?" she beamed, "And your friend?"

"Yes, he's here; just getting a drink."

"Please sit." John accepted the indicated chair.

"Thanks." he muttered self-consciously, willing Barry to appear.

"I wondered where you'd got to... Oh, hello." Barry eyed the girls as though seeing them for the first time. "May I join you?" He asked, flopping onto the chair between John and the brown-eyed girl. "I'm Barry." He announced as Yanna seductively sucked chocolate ice cream from a long-handled spoon. Helga completed the introductions and then muttered something in German that brought a girlish giggle from her companion. Still smiling, she turned towards John.

"It is good for you to find your friend. You are together for many times?" Barry gagged as a swig of beer went with his breath.

"Oh no." He spluttered. "No, we are not together; we are friends but..." Smiling broadly, Yanna measured the last of their wine between the girls' glasses; Barry, sensing a glorious opportunity, waved the empty carafe at a passing waitress.

"No, no please." For an ecstatic instant, Yanna's brown fingers encircled his pale forearm. "It is a long day for us, time for resting." As the fingers fell away from his tingling skin, Helga arose and instigated a brief flurry of hand shaking. Undaunted, Barry played a final card.

"Perhaps we could meet up for a coffee tomorrow... or dinner?"

"Friends are inviting us to a boat, I do not know all the plans." Yanna beamed, following Helga towards the exit.

As the clock in The Waypoint Bar ticket towards midnight, Barry voiced his latest concern.

"First thing tomorrow, we'll sort the bed situation. They already thought we were a couple; where would we be if they knew we shared a bed?"

"I'm not too happy about it either." John remarked, his eyes scanning the winking, swaying mast-lights of the yachts anchored in the marina.

Next morning, John was even less happy about it as he opened the apartment door, shortly before seven o'clock.

"Where were you?" Barry enquired sleepily, not believing his watch. John dropped the rolled-up duvet onto the bed and rubbed his left calf vigorously.

"Trying to sleep on the sun lounger. Bloody mosquitoes!" John growled, itching his right thigh.

"Why?"

"Because, thanks to you snoring, I couldn't get a wink of sleep here. Now will you please go for a walk or something and let me get my head down for a few hours." With a shrug, Barry pulled on a shirt and shorts and marched out into the sunlight.

Along the path, past the Meneghello restaurant, the cicadas were already in full flow. Barry paused for some moments to watch an undersized male blackbird struggle with a giant hairy caterpillar; it was then he noticed the sign for Dionis restaurant. Instantly he increased his pace, reaching the little pier by Sv Kliment chapel as a cabin cruiser was about to cast off. Instinctively, he sprinted the final hundred yards and his effort was rewarded as a red-capped figure waved from the bobbing craft.

As the boat gathered speed, another figure appeared at the stern and, above the hum of the revving engine, lilting female voices chanted towards the shore. The girls' words faded to silence as the vessel disappeared around the point; just then the burning sensation at the base of his neck reminded Barry that he had set out without either head gear or sun block.

John swore softly as Barry emerged from the shower.

"What now; haven't you slept enough?" Barry winced as he towelled a reddening shin.

"You're scorched; come here." John sprang from the bed and grabbed a plastic container. "Stand still!" he ordered, massaging after-sun lotion into the heat below Barry's ginger curls. Finally satisfied, he thrust the bottle into Barry's hands. "Do the rest yourself and don't dream of going out of doors again without protection."

John had news when Barry finally joined him for breakfast in the restaurant.

"They'll have the beds sorted by afternoon. How's the neck?"

"I'll live... and... thanks."

"Good. There's a little sandy beach at Perna, about a kilometre from here. Fancy a stroll?" Barry grabbed a red apple before responding.

"I may as well; the girls will be gone all day. By the way, do you know any German?"

"A bit, why?" Barry bit deep into the fruit before smugly announcing.

"I think I'm in there... with Yanna. They even have a pet name for me. It sounds something like *vice bine*. What does it mean?" John shook his head and endured a further twenty minutes of Barry's amorous ramblings before they noticed the boat in the secluded horseshoe cove.

"It's the girls' boat; it's got a little German flag." Barry squealed as he charged through the patchy scrub before suddenly diving for cover. "Wow," he hissed, "get down." A few feet to the right, John complied as Barry continued. "There are two naked women down there."

"Four." John corrected. "Except for a red baseball cap." His gaze fixed on another pair of girls who stood just below his vantage point. "Oh shit."

"What?" Barry croaked, edging – crab-like – towards John's position.

"They're rubbing oil on each other's..."

"But you rubbed ... "

"Barry, get real. *Weisse Beine* means *white legs*. They were taking the piss, they're..." The words fell on deaf ears; Barry was beyond hearing. A mere twenty feet below, in an all enveloping embrace, tanned and pale bodies seemed to melt into each other before slowly slipping from view beneath a jagged outcrop of shimmering red sandstone...

FULL CYCLE

Mick sighed with relieved exhaustion as another satisfied customer freewheeled downhill towards town. For the previous two weeks, the little workshop beside his cottage had been besieged by a seemingly never ending procession of school children, invoking his intercession to redress the ravages that long summer holidays had wrought on their bicycles. This August, Mick had worked harder than at any time in the five years since his retirement from his fitter's job at the village creamery.

Almost reverently, he wiped each wrench and spanner with an oily rag before returning it to its allotted biscuit tin. Hands clamped to the base of his aching back, he had almost pushed himself fully erect when the slanting rays of the waning sun were suddenly excluded from the narrow doorway. *No,* he thought, not daring to look, *not another one and me already late for my supper.*

"I have it, Mick, I have the new front wheel. Look!" Mick looked and thought, *Ah, Teddy, anyone else but you...*

"So I see, boy, you finally got it, and not before time." Teddy wheeled his bike towards the old man, the new rim gripped like a gleaming trophy in his bramble-scarred hand.

"I've been picking blackberries for McCarthy's shop and they let me have the wheel early. Only two more buckets and it'll be paid for." His hunger forgotten, Mick began to undo the wheel nuts, patting the battered rim through a couple of erratic revolutions before finally slipping the axel free of the fork.

How many hours had he wasted on this particular wheel? How many times had he clamped the rusting metal between his knees while straining hands strove to force it back into some semblance of shape?

"You won't know yourself with this wheel; it'll be like having a new bike." Mick gasped as he fastened the final spoke into position. "The tyre isn't that great either; Let me see... ah yeah, we'll try this one." Teddy stared in wide-eyed silence as the craftsman levered the rubber onto the rim before fitting the wheel and finally flipping the bicycle back onto its freshly inflated tyres.

"Thanks, Mick. How much is that?"

"I'll make a deal with you, Teddy. If I see neither you nor your bike before the end of September, there will be no charge. But if I have to go pulling and dragging at that new wheel before then..." Beaming his thanks, Teddy mounted his bike and faced the hill towards home, muttering softly.

"Like a new bike... just like a new bike!"

Peig's disapproving tone greeted Mick at the scullery door.

"I hope you charged him this time!"

"Ah, sure what could I do? Sure we know she hasn't got it."

"Hah, but she'll be able to afford the bingo tomorrow night." Mick wasn't listening; instead, his mind's eye zoomed across the valley to where a young mother nodded her approval of the improvements to her only child's most prized possession. "And me nearly late for Confession over trying to keep your supper warm; all because of *them*!" The front door slammed. Mick pumped the Tilley lamp to greater efficiency before retrieving his shrivelled fry-up from the oven of the black *Stanley* range. He brewed a fresh pot of tea, soundly cursing the day that his widowed elder sister had returned to the old family home to *do* for her bachelor brother.

"Like you did for poor Jack?" Mick shouted at the front door. "God knows 'twas a happy day for him when his heart gave out!"

Early on the following afternoon, as Mick savoured the second-last swallow of his after-Mass pint, his serenity was shattered by a booming voice in his left ear.

"Put that inside your shirt, Mick." The speaker plonked a fresh pint on the counter.

"Your health, Sam. Mick raised the glass momentarily before finishing his first drink in a single swallow. "What's the occasion?"

"Well, I thought 'twould be cheaper to buy a new bike for my Sonny than be paying you to repair the other old crock.

You won't be getting any more soft money from me." His eyes brightening, Mick craned his neck to meet the gaze of his benefactor.

"What about the old bike?" The question brought a snort of derision from the big man.

"Ah, that's well gone, into the foundation of the new cattle mart. When my Sonny is finished with something; it's finished!" His pride in his firstborn's powers of destruction brought a musical lilt to his guttural tone. "There's no stuff in bikes anymore, not since the war." His meaty paw shook Mick's shoulder as he turned to rejoin his company at the end of the bar.

Mick sampled the new pint, scowling at the thought of what Sonny's discarded bike would have meant to Teddy. *What a waste,* Mick grimaced as the free stout began to curdle in his gut, *and it hardly a year old. A bike like that would have seen young Teddy all the way through secondary school.*

Despite Sam's confidence, Mick saw Sonny's new bicycle sooner than either had expected. Two days later, the old man winced as a tortured engine coughed to silence in his cobblestone yard. Like mirror images of each other, a pair of burly figures erupted from the pick-up and waited expectantly.

"This bloody bike is as useless as the old one!" Sam growled as Mick squinted against the bright sunlight.

"It's bloody worse!" Announced the son, jerking his new bike from the flatbed of the mud-spattered *Bedford.*

"What's wrong with it?" Mick sighed resignedly.

"The back wheel won't turn; it's wedged solid!" The adolescent whined, glancing from one adult to the other. Bemused, Mick appraised the expensive racing bike before raising the back wheel and leaning on a pedal. Nothing. Sonny's pronouncement appeared correct. Mick manipulated the gear controls for a moment before offering his verdict.

"It's the gears; they're jammed. Have you got the maker's guarantee?"

"What, me buy from the main dealers? Robbers, every one of them!" Sam seemed genuinely amused at the thought.

"I'll probably have to replace the whole system; maybe fit something less... less complicated?" Sonny's squeals of complaint were silenced by his father's glare.

"Just give him something that he can manage; it's only a bloody bike!"

"I'll have a go but I'll have to order a new gear system."

"Let me know when it's ready." Seconds later the truck growled from the yard, narrowly missing the young mother and son who laboured against the hill, laden with bags of groceries. Teddy eased his burden to the dust of the byroad and raised a reddened palm in salute. Mick's acknowledging smile lacked the enthusiasm to reach his eyes.

Three days later, Sonny's bike finally repaired, Mick was washing his hands in the basin by the back door when Peig sang out.

"He's here again; you'd better charge him this time." Mick winced as the bar of carbolic soap squirted free of his grasp, narrowly missing a cake of cooling soda bread.

"Who's here?" He countered, in momentary denial of his impending dilemma.

"That Hogan girl's brat; honestly, the gall of some people!" Wordlessly, Mick slipped outside, his eyes misting over as he intercepted his customer at the gable of the house. Both wheels were so badly mangled that the boy had to lift the bike by handlebars and saddle, pausing for breath after each couple of faltering steps.

"Good God, Teddy, don't tell me that you carried it all this way?" Mick stifled an oath.

"No, I got a lift to the cross in Jack Kelly's hay car, I only..."

"Ah, Teddy, 'tis rightly frigged this time." Mick's said sadly. "I'm afraid those wheels will never straighten, even the frame is..."

"I know it can't be fixed." Teddy croaked, wringing his bramble-scarred hands. "I want you to have it... for spare parts... to pay for fitting the wheel." There was no doubting the anguish in the boy's red-rimmed eyes. Mick circled the bike, his head shaking in incredulity.

"How could you do that much damage? Did you drive it off a cliff or something?"

"It wasn't me; 'twas *Samson!*"

"*Samson?* Who's *Samson?*"

"Sonny. You know him: he's *Big Sam's* son! He makes us call him *Samson* but we still call him *Sonny* when he can't hear us." A twinkle briefly brightened Mick's eyes as he marvelled at the boy's resilience.

"Ah, Sam's son! Exactly what happened?" Too late, Mick realised how painful it might prove for Teddy to recount his ordeal; yet again, he had underestimated the pluck of the boy.

"I was picking blackberries near the convent graveyard when Sonny was sneaking in to raid the nuns' orchard. He always picks on me; he threw my bucket of blackberries into the briars and then cycled my bike over the graves until the wheels wouldn't turn anymore. Then he bashed the spokes with a huge rock and then ran away." Digesting the news, Mick nodded absently, wondering what ironic quirk in Sonny's genetic memory should cause him to select Teddy, above all others, to bear the brunt of his malevolence.

"I'll tell you what, Teddy. Why don't I have a better look at the bike later on and see if we can't work something out?"

An hour later, Mick's ritual methodology was disrupted when a white *Morris Oxford* car purred into his yard. With alien negligence, Mick allowed a sprocket to crash against the concrete floor as he strode purposefully towards his visitor. Sam, immaculately attired in a navy suit, eased his bulk from the car. Sam's wife, looking equally resplendent, checked her make-up in the rear-view mirror.

"Well, Mick, what's the story with the bike?"

"The bike is ready to go."

"Good, I'll fix up with you so and Sonny can collect it later. What's the damage?" The builder whistled softly at Mick's figure. "Hah, you wouldn't be taking advantage of me, would you?" He peeled a note from a thick colourful wad and held it towards the old man. Ignoring the money, Mick inched closer to his visitor, his words barely audible.

"There's something else, Sam. It has come to my notice that your Sonny is bullying one of the younger lads..."

"I'm surprised at you, Mick; you know what kids are like, they..." Sam's meaty jowls wobbled over his tight shirt collar.

"It's the Hogan girl's lad. You wouldn't like to see what your son did to that poor child's bicycle." Sam flinched, sneaking a surreptitious glace over his shoulder.

"I'll talk to him." Sam whispered.

"Sam, much and all as I appreciate your custom..."

"Look, I said I'd talk to him."

"God knows, they have it hard enough without..."

"Ok, ok, I'll talk to *her!*" Sam hissed, forcing the ten-shilling note into the breast pocket of Mick's plaid shirt before stomping back to his car.

A few minutes past noon on Saturday, Mick's curiosity was roused by the musical tinkle of a bicycle bell. Seconds later, Teddy cruised into the yard and dismounted from a sparkling red sports bike.

"Look, Mick, look!" The boy called breathlessly. "I've got a new bike and Mum has ordered an electric cooker for when the power comes and..." Nodding, Mick flicked a tiny tear from the corner of his right eye; there was something very special about the natural reaction of a small boy to a surprise present from his father...

UNSEATED

On that fateful Sunday afternoon, had anybody suggested that there was anything romantic about horse racing, I'd probably have throttled him there and then, despite the throbbing pains in my freezing fingers. Not that I am violent by nature – far from it. In fact, there are many race-goers who would regard me as something of a wimp... and dim to boot... and at that moment, I would have readily agreed with them. I mean, what rational person would forsake a warm bed and then drive for nearly three hours on a January morning, just to throw life and limb to the mercy of dozens of iron-shod hooves?

And I wasn't getting any younger. The dreaded mid-thirties were fast approaching: the true age of reason, when invincibility finally yields to fallibility. There had been good days too, even great days, I had once ridden a four-timer at Liscarroll, the pinnacle of my twenty-year career over fences, now a vague memory from a past millennium. I'd been just fifteen then... the age of transition... my rite of passage from pony racing to the maelstrom of the point-to-point circuit.

At the time, it had seemed a natural progression. After a few years of clinging to the manes of coloured ponies at local gymkhanas, the thrill of galloping their larger cousins around flat summer fields and open beaches inevitably fuelled my thirst for the greatest challenge of all: the three-mile steeplechase. It had mattered little that those close to me had worn their teeth trying to impress upon me the difference between steering a seasoned campaigner along a firm path and piloting a skittish novice over a myriad of obstacles in mid-winter muck. No, it wasn't their fault that I had left my warm bed and driven – fasting since before midnight – over icy mountain roads and through villages choked Mass-goers' traffic jams...

I've always known where the blame lies... with none other than our national broadcaster: RTE! Those grainy black-and-white images of Pat Taaffe and *Arkle*, avenging the pain of Kinsale at the Cheltenham Festival... that's what had brought me here, three-quarter way across Munster, on that fateful Sunday morning. I suppose if *Rory's Gold*, my only booked mount at the meeting, hadn't dumped me at the furthest part of the course from my car, I would have gone home, washed my gear and set out again a week later to rejoin the merry-go-round.

In all fairness, it wasn't as if *Rory's Gold* had been the only animal to send me back to earth with a bump, I've had many worse spills. I've had more broken legs than a daddy-longlegs in a cobweb, not to mention collarbones, shoulders, ribs, arms, wrists, vertebrae... I could name more of the human skeletal system than your average hospital intern...

But the bloody TV was relentless. How many years did they replay the triumphs of *L'Escargot* and Tommy Carberry in the build-up to the Aintree Grand National? Many years later, the same Tommy was back in business with his son Paul and *Bobby Joe*. Ted and Ruby Walsh, with *Papillon*, are equally guilty, but why do they saddle Irish horses with French names, anyway? I mean, what's wrong with naming a horse *An Seilide* or *Féile-achán*?

I suppose, deep down, I was proud of their successes, but there were circumstances closer to home that just could not be ignored. *Stormin'* Norman Williamson on *Master Oats* is equally culpable in my downfall. Oh, I'd backed them all right, like I was told to, and enjoyed the celebrations afterwards, and it was great to have some part of Ireland making waves across the water. I could have lived with that... even Jim Fitzgerald's sex life... until the Cork trainers really started to take the piss. Both *Imperial Call* and *Monty's Pass* underlined the talents of Leinster boys Conor O'Dwyer and Barry Geraghty, and then – insult to injury – Jim Culloty, from just down the bloody road, started to rewrite the record books with another locally produced animal! How could I quit with all that going on? I'd raced against them all, beaten them all, lost to them all... I still cherish the day that I was offered a spare ride on what was to become Culloty's Gold Cup hero, *Best Mate*!

I didn't take that ride, I couldn't because I'd been already engaged by Tim-Joe, my regular *guv'nor*, to ride something whose name I can't recall, but I do remember being in contention with the future Cheltenham legend when we came to grief at the second last. *Unseated* was how the course commentator had described it. *Unseated*, the term most dreaded by all riders... the word that rang around the course when I parted company with *Rory's Gold*... *Unseated*, the very word that my then girlfriend had used when I'd refused to attend her brother's wedding on the day before my final fling.

"*Have it your way,*" she'd said, "*but as far as I'm concerned you can consider yourself stood-down, jocked-off, unseated... whatever!*" In fairness, I suppose I could have attended the wedding in Dublin and still got back in time for my race on the following day, but she had begun to nag me about my race riding... and... you know what the song says: '*going to a wedding is the making of another.*'

To this day, I still maintain that *run-out* would have been a more accurate description of *Rory's Gold's* exit from that race. I mean, what do people expect? The point-to-point scene is all about introducing young inexperienced animals to the discipline of competition. How many people do you know who would climb aboard a half-tonne of nervous energy and attempt to nurse it through three miles of mud and fifteen huge fences?

Look at it from a horse's point of view: up to a few short months before, that youngster would have known nothing but freedom. The freedom of open fields, the freedom to run in whatever direction it might choose, freedom from bit, bridle and boot, but mostly freedom from the terrifying concept of a predator clinging to its back. Yes, predators are what we are, that's why our eyes are fixed on the front of our faces, just like cats, dogs, lions and the like. Where are a horse's eyes? Yes, at the sides of its head, like a rabbit or a sheep or an antelope... that's why our kind has spent centuries developing various gadgets to stifle an equine's natural instinct to flee at the first hint of an approach from the rear. Winkers, blinkers, visors, cheek pieces... call them what you like... that's what they are all for: to curb an animal's primeval urge to flee.

We've all seen those wildlife programmes; you know, where the lion or leopard leaps onto the zebra's back. Every horse has a zebra in its genetic memory and, let's face it, our kind take more prey in a single day than all the lions in Africa would take in a year. While it's obvious that the zebra's survival depends on shaking that lion or leopard from its back, it needs to be pointed out that every sinew and fibre of a horse's being screams at him to respond in exactly the same way. To this day, I'm convinced that it was that zebra that caused my departure from the saddle on my final day in the business.

Come to think of it, Tim-Joe wasn't entirely blameless either. Originally a dairy farmer, Tim-Joe had caught the bug when he'd discovered that an odd point-to-point meeting could relieve the monotony of rural bachelor life during the hurling off-season. Within a year, he'd bought his first brood mare and, by the time I first encountered him, a couple of decades later, he was breeding about a dozen foals a year. By then his milking days were well over, but he did keep about thirty suckling cows along with the forty-or-so horses that roamed his two-hundred acres of pristine land near the Tipperary border.

"For fear of the frost." Jim-Joe would quip whenever his cattle were mentioned. *"Horses are all very fine: they're great fun and you could be lucky, but you can always depend on the cows to pay the bills."* To paraphrase Ted Walsh, Tim-Joe was once of those perfectionists who'd have his charges *schooled to the eyeballs* before they'd ever appear in public. Yes, Tim-Joe's talent was renowned and respected by jumping people on both sides of the channel.

I was already attired in Jim-Joe's colours when his battered jeep rattled to a halt beside my Audi.

"A new one?" I asked, getting my first glimpse of the unfamiliar chestnut rump above the tailboard of the single horsebox.

"Wait 'til you see." He winked, lowering the ramp and backing my latest mount from its conveyance. It was there again: the excitement, the anticipation: this could be the one that would finally get me to Cheltenham or Aintree or Galway or Listowel or any place where they raced *inside the rails*. This animal had everything: height, scope, athleticism, muscle and, most important of all, those large unblinking eyes that mirrored the courage and character within.

"Is he as good as he looks?" I finally managed.

"Better! He's the best I've ever handled!" Tim-Joe grinned, tightening the girths.

"Can he win?" I asked, stifling an involuntary shudder.

"He could... easily... but he won't!" My surprise must have showed. "He's been bought... he's off to England at the end of the week. I had to beg them to let me run him today."

"All the more reason to go at it full tilt!" I countered.

"They want him kept under wraps; that's why I want you to ride him. If I put a young lad up, he'd be tempted to go for glory. Just hunt him around and let as many as possible finish in front of you. The next time you'll see him it'll be on television at Cheltenham. Bar a heat wave, he'll piss the bumper. I know you're disappointed but... Back him as soon as possible; he'll be a huge price ante-post. If he doesn't land the gamble, I'll cover your stake."

If I'd had any doubts about Tim-Joe's confidence in the newcomer, they had dissipated by the time we'd jumped the second: *Rory's Gold* had it all. We cruised for about a mile, taking the scenic route on the wide outside. *Rory* behaved like the perfect gentleman, I could feel Tim-Joe's gifted hands in his mouth. Then the pacemakers began to thin out, I'd heard some fallers behind but I was determined to live or die by that ageless maxim I'd first heard early in my gymkhana days: *never, ever look back*! But soon a new fear seized me, was there anything in the field capable of finishing in front of us? With a mile to go we were an improving third, and my mount was only beginning to warm up.

Shit. I thought in a brief moment of madness, *I'll never again sit on an animal as good as this... let's go out in a blaze of glory Everybody everywhere will know who rode him to his first win... my name will be forever associated with his.*

Then I thought of Tim-Joe's words...

"I had to beg them to let me run him today." Reality check: if it weren't for Tim-Joe's contacts, I wouldn't have a car to bring me here, a house to go home to, or a job to keep everything ticking over.

Shit! We were in the lead and cantering. Approaching the back straight I got serious; I shoved my weight onto his withers, flung the stirrups forward and hauled hard against his head. This is why I blame Tim-Joe: that poor horse had never been stopped before; he had no idea what was happening. First one and then his other eye turned towards me... and then he saw something he'd never seen before... an animal attacking from the rear...

No, it wasn't me; I could hear the hooves of the only other horse still seriously in the race. As the next fence loomed before us, I could feel my arms being dragged from their sockets, but this wasn't just any fence, this was the huge double ditch. At this speed we had no chance of clearing it; I pulled again, slipped my feet free of the stirrups and, sitting-dead weight in the saddle, pressed the soles of my boots against his elbows... hoping to shorten his stride.

For an instant I could feel the challenger's breath on my elbow... *Rory's Gold* took off before the wings, cleared the fence with at foot to spare, landed galloping with a four length lead, took a quick glance with his left eye and promptly did a handbreak turn to the right. I found myself pedalling through thin air, onto the very spot where our host landowner had been foddering his bullocks all through the winter. Oh, yes... isn't this where you came in? Anyway, once free of all predators, *Rory's Gold* gave me a disdainful look before casually cantering back towards his transport.

Tim- Joe and *Rory's Gold* were probably halfway home by the time I'd reached my car. My long-overdue breakfast consisted of a cardboard ham sandwich, a bottle of water and a huge dollop of bitter realisation. It was all over for me and yet

I felt privileged, I'd just ridden the finest animal that I would ever sit on and I also knew that, even if he didn't go on to win the bumper this year, there would be a few nice hurdle races to come before he'd fulfil his true potential and claim the most coveted prize in National Hunt racing: the Gold Cup itself.

Somebody was banging at my window; I lowered it slowly and found myself face-to-face with an adversary from my early days.

"Are you riding in the last?" He asked, businesslike as ever.

"No!" I growled, starting my engine.

"Tim-Joe said you might do me... ah... him a favour. My young lad dislocated his shoulder in your race... "

"Sorry, Hugh, I'm going home." I started to turn my steering wheel.

"It's her last race, I'm putting her in-foal... With you up, she'd have a good outside chance..."

About an hour later, Hugh gave me the leg-up onto a nondescript, mousy-bay mare. His instructions were simple...

"She has a mind of her own. If she doesn't want it, don't force her, but if she's game, give her full tilt. Good luck!" *Her last race? Full tilt?* Why not?

Going down to the start, she reminded me of myself, facing the office on an average Monday morning: that sort of reluctant acceptance of the inevitable. She jumped-off willingly enough, settled quickly and seemed to handle the ground well. She took her fences economically and, with a circuit to go, I knew that we'd go close. She scrubbed across the last before the straight in third place, about two lengths behind a compact grey gelding on a tight rein. The long-time leader was coming back to us and remembering *Rory's* zebra, I chanced a backward glance. There was no lion or leopard, no cat of any description and certainly no horse capable of worrying my mouse.

At the second-last we were a clear second and, from the way the punters were shouting, there was a lot of money riding on one of us. I was about to change my hands in preparation for the final obstacle when the little mare took the bit between her teeth. We cleared the fence upsides as the decibels increased from the enclosure... The commentator's distorted voice kept repeating two names and then I realised that I had no idea of what my mount was called. As the winning post flashed by, I genuinely believed that we were ahead but the punters' groans sowed the tiniest seeds of doubt in my mind. On the way back to the enclosure, I sneaked a look at the number cloth beneath the saddle, just as the announcer called the result. We had won, I was going out in a blaze of glory after all.

After much backslapping and the compulsory photo-shoot, Hugh pressed some banknotes into my hand and invited me to join the winning connections back at the village hotel.

Hotel, I thought, *bath, food, drink, bed... Monday morning?* But I didn't have to work on Monday morning; I didn't have to work for two whole weeks. Neither did I have to fly to The Algarve on Tuesday... I'd been *"stood-down, jocked-off, unseated... whatever!"* And, I had an unexpected bonus in my back pocket.

My host's entourage departed shortly after the meal. Reluctantly, I gave my mobile number to Hugh but was quite adamant about my retirement. There was a pleasant buzz in the residents' bar; the party who'd won *Rory's* race insisted that I take a sip from the cup. Finally, I found a quiet corner at the end of the bar and ordered a pint.

"That's on me!" A musical voice chimed from behind my right ear. I started to protest. "No!" She insisted. "It's the least I can do! I'm Julie, *Billy The Bookie's* daughter. I was in charge of the pitch today and held far too much money on that good-thing that you beat. You saved me big-time! Won't you join us, please?" I took a closer look at my benefactor. She was neither tall nor slim, with a wholesome rustic face that beamed through an unruly mop of blonde curls. In her baggy green sweater, jeans and wellingtons, she was the very antithesis of my ex and the similar stick insect types that I'd been pursuing since adolescence. "There's room here." She smiled, patting the seat beside her. Instead of excuses, I offered my name and my hand, and sat.

Tim-Joe isn't often wrong but his prediction that I'd watch *Rory's Gold* win the Cheltenham bumper on TV was well wide-of-the-mark. I did take his advice and plunged my Portuguese holiday money, on-the-nose, at 66/1... No, Tim-Joe didn't re-fund my stake; he didn't have to... We both watched *Rory's Gold* romp home – in the flesh – from his owner's private box in Prestbury Park... with my girlfriend Julie. Sure, you know Julie, she's *Billy The Bookie's* daughter...

CHECKING OUT

During all of my years in both school and college, I could never quite understand the compulsive desire of certain individuals to scratch their initials into items of other people's property. Nowadays, the aerosol can seems to have replaced the crucifix of the rosary beads, the humble horse-nail or the more sophisticated penknife, as the instrument of choice of those wishing to leave their mark behind for posterity. While still a child, I had resolved make my mark in a more significant and enduring way.

What had fascinated me most were the brass plates of the various professionals in town: doctors, veterinary surgeons, solicitors, accountants and the like. None of your *T O'S*, *J McC* or *B G* business for me; I mean, who was *B G* anyway? Bob Geldof? I don't think so. *T A*, however, I had my suspicions about; Teresa Andrews, a native of the town, was our primary school principal, and had been a classmate of my mother's. After a little detective work, I was certain that it all fitted together, because *T A* hadn't just left her initials; she had also scratched a date and the following words: *goodbye to this old dump forever...* Well, I suppose, that's life... and death.

A few weeks ago, the town said goodbye to the old school building. *The Minister for Education*, herself a former pupil, marked the official opening of its successor by unveiling a bronze torch-of-learning plaque in the school's foyer, dedicated to Teresa's memory. The *old dump* had seen Teresa out.

Some six weeks before the new school was opened and eighteen months short of her retirement date, Teresa's body was discovered in the hallway of her home. Initial reports had suggested that she'd suffered a stroke, fallen down the stairs and broken her neck.

Although an only child and a spinster to boot, Teresa had the biggest send-off ever seen in the parish. Her forty-plus years of service to the generations of young minds who'd sat before her, was reflected in the throngs that had huddled outside the gates of the crammed church, in September rain. They had come from every county, scores of countries and five continents. Yes, *T A* had left her mark all right.

Not that I can claim any personal credit for being there, it was work that caused my presence... that, and the diligence of a young GP, yet another graduate of Teresa's academy. I don't know what came over me; perhaps, it had something to do with actually checking into the hotel: the hotel that I had always considered to be the preserve of my betters and well beyond the aspirations of simple townsfolk like me.

The instant I set foot in that room, I felt an almost uncontrollable urge to leave my mark in it... somewhere. My mobile rang, I muttered an apology, grabbed my case and headed for the car park. Strictly speaking, the morgue of the regional hospital should have been my first port of call, but I'd reasoned that, if Teresa's mortal remains had already waited for nearly thirty hours, another thirty minutes wasn't going to make a whole lot of difference. Yes, it was because of Teresa that I was back in my hometown... and the fact that young Gillian Kiely G. P. had requested a post mortem into our mentor's unexpected death.

Eight hours later, I finished my solitary meal in the hotel dining room, only vaguely aware of the banter of my erstwhile colleagues from the adjoining public bar. This was one problem that I hadn't foreseen prior to my recent surprise elevation in status. Suddenly, *I* was that angel of death, the vulture descending to desecrate the corpse, to the horror of the bereaved, to the chagrin of local police and the hostility of all would-be suspects – likely or not. As fifth assistant to the *State Pathologist*, the most field action I could have reasonably expected would have been an occasional call-out during the peak holiday season. Now, thanks to an attack of gout, a difficult pregnancy, a femur fractured on a football pitch, a hush-hush spell in rehab and a honeymoon, I found myself in charge of my third case in less than a fortnight.

My baptism of fire – well, blood actually – had been back in Dublin. It had proved a straightforward stabbing case, complete

with the murder weapon still in the chest of the victim and con-
veniently covered with the fingerprints of a long-suffering wife.
The new widow had been only too willing to put her hands
up and confirm, in addition to her intent, motive and opportunity, her satisfaction in a job well done. That had been just
twelve days before and, afterwards, I had simply driven back to
my apartment, opened a bottle of wine and watched a DVD. A
drink, that's what I needed now. With a last wistful glance at
the dessert menu, I wandered into the hotel lounge.

After a disappointing perusal of the bar's wine stocks, I decided to settle for a fruity Australian red, which I brought to an
armchair in the front lobby, beside a street-facing bay window.
Although I had grown up in town, I no longer had any family
there. Both of my brothers were now married abroad and, after
Mum's death seven years before, Dad had gone to live with a
widowed sister back in his native Cork. So there I was, an in-
sider looking out of my hotel window, an outsider looking in at
my past.

It was that time of evening when streets experience a little
final flurry of pre-dusk activity. As I recalled the names behind the ageing faces that chatted their way home from evening
Mass, a wave of nostalgia swelled in my throat. Occasionally,
a furtive glance from a driver who might have dallied for more
than just *the one*, reminded me that it wasn't just the worship-
pers who had aged.

Then I saw her; even after almost two decades there was no
mistaking the catwalk strut of those lithe supermodel limbs,
propelled by confidence and vivacity. And that hair: waving
tresses of burnished copper, rebounding from her collarbones
as though spring-loaded... Rachel had stood out even in primary school: bright, precocious, wilful and loved by all... well,
almost all...

She had been my very first best friend. We were classmates,
neighbours and, as neither of us had a sister and both our dads
were policemen, it was inevitable that we should play together.
It was on my seventh birthday that I'd visited Rachel to show off
my first bike. She didn't have a bike but was well able to cycle,

so I let her have a good go on mine, around the little grassy plot behind her house. As I was just learning and wasn't really able to steer and pedal at the same time, I needed the occasional push to keep mobile.

At the edge of the lawn, there was a drop of about six feet into an old drain, then concealed beneath a profusion of summer growth. By my third lap, I felt that Rachel was really warming to her role... Suddenly, I was going too fast, but, before I could get my feet to the ground, Rachel gave a mighty heave and down I went, bike and all, into a tangle of nettle and briar.

Rachel had almost reached my window now; she was smiling... greeting someone... a woman... a younger woman. Had I seen that woman in Galway last week? *Galway*, I just couldn't get Galway out of my mind... even during my examination of Teresa's body... but how could it be? What possible connection could there have been between a twenty-eight year old Galway nurse and my old schoolteacher?

"Excuse me, hello." It was Rachel's friend.

"Yes?" What else could I say?

"Sorry for disturbing you, but didn't I see you in Galway last week?"

"Yes, you might have..."

"Are you the pathologist?" I nodded. "May I?" She indicated the chair opposite.

"Please do, I was just going."

"No." She took a half step towards me, as if about to restrain me in my seat. "I... I mean, please don't... I need to talk you. I'm Karen, Karen Shields."

"The journalist?" I asked, recognising the name. "I'm sorry but I can't talk to you. If you contact the press office..."

"I don't want to question you; it's about Mandy Joyce, the girl who died in Galway, she was... we were..."

"I am so sorry, but..."

"Mandy was the fourth lesbian – that I know of – to die in mysterious circumstances, since last June..." That got my attention.

"Four? Who...?"

111

"I've got the details back at my B&B... If you have the time..." She arose and hovered uncertainly. I downed my wine in a single gulp and found myself saying,

"This has to be totally off-the-record. If a single word appears in print..."

"It won't, I promise. This isn't just another story; this is personal!"

An hour later, back in the privacy of my room, my laptop was working overtime. It was soon evident that Karen had done her homework: four young women had died unexpectedly and four different pathologists – including me – had carried out their autopsies. While I couldn't speak for three of the cases, I knew for an absolute fact that none of my colleagues had expressed more than a casual interest in my findings regarding Mandy Joyce's death. Now, thanks to a bereaved journalist, it seemed that at least four victims were connected: not only had all four women been in same-sex relationships, but toxicology tests had revealed unusually high levels of *Diazepam* in all four bodies. *Jesus,* a shiver ran through me, *surely it couldn't be? Still...* I grabbed my phone and dialled.

Dr. Kiely was actually in the hotel when she received my call. Two minutes later, her face was a maze of questions when I joined her in the residents' lounge. She handed me a brandy balloon and indicated a pair of armchairs in the far corner.

"I thought we could both do with a proper drink. If you don't like brandy, I guarantee you that it won't go to waste." I shook my head and took a sip.

"It's perfect." I assured her, easing into the plush leather chair. "Cheers!"

"Cheers! Yes, I did prescribe *Diazepam* for Teresa, but you surely can't think that the cases are linked."

"Because Teresa was old and straight?" My question was rewarded with a splutter as Gillian's drink went with her breath.

"Straight? I thought you knew..." It was my turn to gag.

"You mean...?"

"I thought everybody knew; the whole town has known for years..." Her giggle was infectious.

"Who...?"

"Miss Baker."

"Miss Baker, the little lady who sold the holy pictures and the statues?"

"And the First Communion missals and the rosary beads... Yes, even in this little town!"

"But, didn't Miss Baker spend some time in the nuns?" Another giggle.

"That's where their nickname came from, and from the matching navy anoraks that they always wore on their walks: *The sisters of the hood*!" Gillian's phone chimed. She pulled a face and composed herself before answering. After a few *OKs, all rights* and *u-hums*, she finished with a single *thanks*, then took a long deep breath and released it slowly before fixing me with a steady gaze.

"That was the hospital. Teresa's bloods are back and yes, your hunch was correct: *Diazepam*, an awful lot of *Diazepam*... too much to have come from her own prescription."

So Teresa *had* been murdered, as had the young Galway nurse who had been found floating in the Claddagh and three other young women of whom I knew nothing, except for their sexual orientation. Was Karen Shields now also a target and, if so, who else? There were already five dead women, in four different counties, all with huge doses of *Diazepam*. It had to be a serial killer – a very mobile serial killer – one who disapproved of same-sex relationships...

Or, could it be another lesbian, one whose advances had been spurned by all the victims? I instantly dismissed the thought: Teresa had been in her sixties, decades older than the others... so where did she fit in the big picture? For that matter, where did any of us fit?

During breakfast next morning, Head Office phoned. The staff shortage had eased and my request for a few days' leave had been granted, on condition that I would remain within the State – on stand-by – just in case of emergencies. While the iron was hot, I requested copies of my colleagues' reports on the other deaths and arranged for a senior Garda to accept my call from my temporary office at the hospital. Less than an hour later, my pulse raced at the sound of the Assistant Commissioner's voice on the line. Anticipation soon cooled to despair, he was adamant that there was no forensic evidence to connect the cases.

Apparently, Mandy Joyce had accidentally drowned following a high intake of alcohol and prescription drugs. The death of the young couple in a Dublin apartment was due to an apparent suicide pact, following their families' disapproval of their relationship, and the young sales rep, whose car had crashed near Athlone, had merely fallen asleep at the wheel following a weekend of serious partying. As for Teresa, she had simply fallen down her stairs and broken her neck, having misjudged her dosage of *Diazepam*. He did assure me, however, that there were still some toxicology tests outstanding and, should any new evidence emerge, any – or all – of the cases would be reinvestigated, even to the extent of ordering exhumations.

Badly in need of cheering-up, I decided to invite Gillian to dinner but alas, she had a previous engagement. The wave of isolation that washed over me was like nothing I'd ever experienced before. Here I was, a stranger in an anonymous hotel room in my hometown. Another thirty-something, without family or friends, with nothing to show for my life except cases full of plastic white suits and grotesque sharp instruments and a string of failed relationships, one of which continued to be the source of great pain...

Pain? Karen Shields was in pain; perhaps she could use some company too. I was wrong: from the way that Karen answered her phone I instantly realised that she was feeling no pain. She'd had lunch with a friend and had gone overboard on the wine. She had just recently returned to her B&B and was about to take a nap but thought that she might resurface for a nightcap later.

As it happened, my after-dinner company was provided by an unlikely source. As I was leaving the dining room, I literally bumped into Rachel. My instinctive apology was stifled by her fierce hug.

"It is you, my God! Come on, let's have a drink, we've got a lot of catching up to do." I allowed myself to be led by the arm into the main bar.

"Rachel, you look wonderful!" I stated the obvious. She half-turned and flashed me a smile that bore testament to the success of the braces that had been the bane of her teen years. I opted for wine; Rachel ordered a gin and tonic.

"You're here for the funeral?"

"Yes." I nodded, taking a sip of wine to dilute my lie.

"God, I can't believe it. They've come from all over! But of course, you were always one of her favourites... except when we played *Cagney and Lacy*... You're a doctor now, aren't you?"

"Yes." I deliberately kept it as vague as possible. "And you're a nurse?" She gave me that old condescending look.

"My nursing days are long past. I was never cut out for bed pans and puke... no offence intended, Doctor." My smile was genuine enough; I had never considered her nursing material in the first place.

"So what do you do these days?" She glanced over both shoulders before leaning closer; I could smell her perfume, her hair...

"I peddle drugs." She whispered throatily. My surprise was mostly feigned. "Not that kind of drugs; legal ones!" This time I was genuinely surprised but responded with an exaggerated sigh of relief.

"Whew! You're a company rep?" I could see that she still delighted in teasing me.

"I'm with *Pharmaveld*." She announced, picking up her handbag. "Coming out for a smoke? Oops... I suppose not!"

"Actually, I really should be going," I lied, finishing my wine with an un-ladylike gulp. "It's been great meeting you, Rachel, next time the drinks are on me."

"I'll hold you to that." She was already on her way to the door. I toyed with the idea of phoning Karen again but, deciding against it, ordered another glass of wine and retired to my room.

I had just finished breakfast when my phone rang; the caller introduced himself as Detective Inspector Ryan and he informed me that he wished to meet with me urgently. Wondering how he'd got my number, I almost choked on my last mouthful of tea when the detective entered the dining room and marched directly to my table.

"That was fast." My quip made little impression on his stony features.

"Doctor," he said formally, ignoring my invitation to sit, "did you phone Karen Shields last night?"

"Yes, at about eight o'clock..."

"Four minutes past, to be precise. Why did you phone her?"

"I invited her for a drink but she was about to take a nap..."

"You didn't actually meet her so?"

"No, I..."

"Have you ever been to her B&B?"

"Yes... once... but what's this all about?"

"When she didn't report for breakfast, her landlady went to check on her and found her dead. Where were you between eight o'clock last night and now?"

"Am I a suspect?"

"Doctor, please... It looks as though you were the last person to speak to her, even if it was on a mobile phone and you've admitted to being to her B&B... I just want to eliminate you from..."

"I was here... in the dining room until about nine-thirty, then I had a drink in the bar with an old acquaintance – until about ten – and then I went to my room, where I stayed until breakfast."

"Can anybody verify that?"

"I was online until after midnight. In fact, I exchanged several e-mails with a colleague in Dublin. I'm sure you'll be able to track my movements in cyberspace." He seemed to relax.

"Thank God for that," he almost smiled, "and thank you for your time, Doctor."

"I suppose you'll want me at the scene." I said, getting to my feet.

"Well, no... actually, they're sending somebody Dublin. Your office thought that you might be too close to this one." *Christ*, I thought after the detective had left, *I am a suspect*. With frustration-fuelled resolve, I returned to my room and opened my laptop.

As luck would have it, the pathologist who had been assigned to Karen's case was the young man who was my immediate senior and with whom I had an excellent rapport. He returned my call immediately after concluding his preliminary examination and readily agreed to join me at the hotel. Even though he declined my invitation to dinner in favour of returning to the morgue, he did leave me in a better frame of mind than that in which he had found me. At least, I now felt that there was somebody else who was willing to consider the potential enormity of the situation.

After Teresa's removal to the parish church, I partook of another solitary meal and then decided to do something that I hadn't done since my graduation: go for a pub-crawl around town. My instincts had proved correct, the town was buzzing with old school friends. It was almost like the Christmases of my college years: it seemed that everybody had come home. My first drink was a very quick one: I bumped into the Sheehan sisters just as they were about to leave my first watering hole to meet up with the rest of their gang. Accepting their invitation to join them, I ordered a small vodka and orange and threw it straight back. We were on our way.

Two pubs later, we were seven strong and determined to paint the town red. Then my heart sank: Rachel had spotted us. Within minutes it was obvious that all of the girls were in awe of her, they hung onto her every word and readily agreed with her most outlandish comments. Then it happened.

"Isn't that Sandra O'Toole, over by the pool table?" I asked of nobody in particular.

"Has she got the little wife with her?" Rachel grinned and I then noticed that Sandra was indeed accompanied by a plain little creature, with lank mousy hair and protruding teeth. Rachel's glare was one of cold blue steel.

"Disgusting cunts!" She spat. "I'm not staying here to watch that carry-on; who's with me?" Despite a few murmurs of *'live and let live'* and *'it's their own business'*, drinks were finished with inappropriate haste and our troop was back on the crawl.

While one of the Sheehan girls ordered our next round, I forced my way to Rachel's side.

"Were you serious back there, about Sandra O'Toole?" She looked at me aghast.

"Serious? That little dyke was at it even when we were in secondary school, she almost tried it on with me at the Christmas hop."

"That isn't what I meant. If she is that way inclined, so what? This is the twenty-first century."

"Ah, you've burnt your bra too, have you? Well, Doctor, whether it's the first century or twenty-first, it's still an abomination. What about Romans 1:26-27? *'For even their women exchanged the natural use of what is against nature...and receiving in themselves the penalty of their error which was due.'* Or Revelations 2:21: *'And I gave her time to repent of her sexual immorality, and she did not repent.'* So, Doctor, what do you say to that... or perhaps I should call you *the sister of death...?*" I felt as though my colon had frozen solid but I forced my dirtiest belly laugh.

"Good on you, Rachel, always the right answer at the right time." Somebody handed us our drinks. "Cheers!" I clinked my glass against Rachel's and was rewarded with a knowing smirk.

"Cheers... *sister!*" At her obvious scorn, I went weak at the knees. It was difficult to contemplate, yet Rachel ticked all the boxes: she had unlimited access to all types of drugs, she was constantly crisscrossing the country and she believed that the only good lesbian was a dead one. I had never been more certain of anything in all of my life and, if Rachel knew what I thought she knew, then we both knew that she had identified her next target.

It was as though we had psychically agreed a demilitarised zone: despite the constant milling of bodies in our corner of the crowded bar, there always seemed to be at least two neutral pawns between us. Suddenly Rachel slipped a cigarette from her bag.

"Who's with me?" She waved the cigarette in a circling motion above her head. All responded except the Sheehan girls.

"Hold on!" I hadn't realised that I'd shouted; they turned back as one. "My round, the same for everyone?"

"Not for me!" Rachel said.

"Go on, go on, go on!" Mentally, I joined the chorus.

"Ok so, but this is my last. I'm on the road in the morning, so it's across the street to bed after this!" She turned with a swish of iridescent hair. The Sheehan sisters were also on the move – to the bathroom – and I was left alone in crowd of preoccupied strangers.

The Sheehan girls were first to return, just as I ferried the last glass of *Guinness* to our table. I delegated my handbag-minding duties and rushed towards the toilet, I badly needed to pee and didn't really fancy leaving my drink unsupervised in Rachel's presence.

Rachel did leave after my round, muttering something about us making sure that the old cow got put in the ground. After Rachel's departure, I suggested that we should wind up our session back at my hotel. The Sheehan girls opted for home, but the rest of us slipped past the disapproving glare of the doorman, seconds before closing time.

"We're residents," I sad, waving my room key, "I'm in 207." We adjourned to a little room at the rear of the residents' lounge, and it soon became clear that Rachel's absence had done wonders for the mood of our group. The atmosphere was suddenly less charged... laid-back even, and the prettiest girl in the bunch was sitting right next to me. I hadn't met her before that night, she was a friend of the younger Sheehan girl, younger than most of us...

"What was that Rachel one on about... earlier I mean?" She asked, meeting my gaze full on.

"I suppose she has her hang-ups, lots of people do..." I shrugged dismissively; her eyes never flickered.

"She was quoting scripture..." I stared into her dark pools of temptation.

"I seem to remember scripture saying something about casting stones too..."

"I think I need a smoke, would you..."

"No... I..."

"...have one with me?" An eyelid fluttered, causing a tiny fragment of mascara to fall and rest on the curve of her left cheekbone. I swallowed hard, rose light-headedly and followed her through the doorway.

After Teresa's burial, we returned to my room for a proper goodbye. Afterwards, despite our silent acceptance of the inevitable, we went through the formality of exchanging phone numbers before finally parting. A further twenty minutes saw me packed and ready for the road back to Dublin. I was just about to do a final check of the room when a blaring siren drew me to the open street window.

As I leaned through to watch the police car slide to a screaming halt, I did a quick calculation... Yes, that building would be directly opposite the pub where Rachel had abandoned us... A glance at the post office clock reminded me that it was past my checkout time. By now, they must have realised that they should be searching for a serial killer.

Mentally, I reviewed my alibi, as I've done many times in the subsequent months... I had six solid witnesses, all of whom had seen Rachel leave our company, and I had two more who were absolutely unbreakable: one surly night porter who would confirm my time of entry to the hotel and one devoted dark-eyed girl who would swear that I hadn't left her side until well after noon on the following day.

For certain, not one of them had seen me hold a half-pint glass between my knees, beneath a table, while I broke open a succession of *Diazepam* capsules and stirred the powder into Rachel's lager with the straw from my own *black Russian* cocktail. On impulse, I removed the copy of *Gideon's Holy Bible* from my bedside locker and wrote the day's date at the top of page 997, above the words: *Then He said to her, "For this say-*

ing go your way; the demon has gone out of your daughter."
Mark 7:29...

Best Man

"I'm not going and that's that. None of your family ever liked me anyway. Besides, I have too much to do here; just look at all this ironing." She had pointed to the few pairs of knickers, bras and other oddments that were strewn across the hall radiator.

What was she really trying to tell me? He pondered, nearing the hotel after the sixty-mile drive from his home. Recalling some of the occasions when he'd almost walked away, he sighed. Surely, there had to be more to life than just going through the motions; even God would have to admit that two people finding happiness apart made more sense than they living together in misery.

Yet, his hopes had soared anew when, almost six months before, she had finally agreed to begin trying for a baby. Something akin to a second honeymoon had followed before the old patterns and cracks began to reappear. Her last-minute refusal to attend his only sibling's wedding, despite having spent a weekend away shopping for an outfit, was the most recent in a series of sickening blows. Once again, he was forced to ask himself if starting a family was such a good idea after all.

He almost enjoyed the rehearsal, even if the jokes of the young priest had varied little from those of his counterpart, on a similar occasion, over a decade before. Afterwards, back at the hotel, he nodded and smiled bravely to the questioning glances of relatives and acquaintances, occasionally responding to more direct enquiries with his standard white lie. *After all*, he reasoned, *'doing the ironing' didn't have quite the same impact as 'the time of the month'*. Not that it mattered anyway: this occasion was all about Brenda and tomorrow would be the biggest day of his baby sister's life.

"Cheer up, we're here for a wedding; not a funeral." The dark haired girl's words scythed through his wandering thoughts.

"I suppose." He shrugged, pretending to focus on the muted lips of the *Sky News* reporter on the distant TV screen.

"You're Brenda's brother; aren't you... the best man?"

"Yeah... the best man." He drained his glass.

"I work with Brenda. We are all so excited; she's the first of the gang to take the plunge."

Why don't you just go away? He wanted to scream but, seeing her properly, said.

"Don't worry, you have plenty of time... I mean... Sorry; will you excuse me?" He rose abruptly and headed towards the exit... and solitude.

He had almost cleared the lobby when a familiar voice halted him in his tracks.

"You're not leaving already?" Concern shone in Brenda's blue eyes. He paused, allowing her arms to encircle his waist.

"No, no. I just thought I'd take a look at the old town."

"I'm so glad you're here." She hugged him towards her.

"I couldn't miss *your* wedding. I'm so happy for you; he seems like a great guy."

"Oh yes, he really is. What about... will she...?" She steered him towards a quiet corner.

"No, ah..."

"There's no need to explain. *You* are here and that's all that matters. You are all the family that I need. And don't worry, you don't have to hang around... afterwards."

"Thanks, we'll see. I'll catch you later, I..." He gestured towards the door. After another quick cuddle, she released him to the awaiting darkness.

The first half of his life had been spent in this town. Now, as he aimlessly ambled the once-familiar footpaths, he shivered. Whether it was due to the biting March wind or a touch of *déjá vu* was immaterial; these days, regardless of where he went, he was a stranger. On impulse, he turned into an off-licence to buy a pack of cigars and a disposable lighter.

She wouldn't approve of this, he mused lighting up, *what she doesn't know won't worry her.* Continuing on his pilgrimage of nostalgia, he had almost finished his cigar when sounds of other days halted him in his tracks. Taking a final puff, he dropped the stub down a gutter grill and opened the pub door.

He paused and stared, feeling as though he had stepped back in time.

The timeless aromas of hemp, leather and animal feed-rations continued to vie with those of paraffin and linseed oil. Greyhound leads, muzzles, bridles, mouthpieces and bicycle tyres all hung within pint-raising distance of the drinkers. Over the years, he had boasted of the scene to incredulous city ears, of being able to buy anything from a side of home-cured bacon to a turf *sleán* in his local pub. How many times had embarrassment prevented him from revealing this aspect of his past to sophisticated visiting friends?

The bacon counter was long gone but he was fairly certain that a *sleán* or two could still be unearthed from the little tool store at the rear of the premises. It was a strange world: what had been dismissed as old-fashioned a lifetime ago was now considered trendy in some quaint retro way.

It's the same with the music, he concluded, listening to the forgotten melodies. *Father Kelly's, St. Anne's, The Foxhunter's...* he mouthed each name as the opening notes fine-tuned his memory. The faces of the players might change but the music played on, as if it had a life of its own.

After the reel-set had come to a climactic end, he ordered a pint of stout from a blonde girl with a glittering *diamante* nose stud. Returning his attention to the session, he took a deep breath and then released it with a whistling hiss.

God, he thought, *I used to be the youngest in the session; now I'd be the oldest. Where was I when my hey-day came and went?*

"It's on the house... Give us a song!" Surely, the gravelly voice wasn't directed at him? "Go on, for old-time's sake!"

It couldn't be. His mind racing, he turned to meet the speaker's knowing wink. *Take away some weight, add some hair, darken it, add a beard...it is!* The pumping handshake over, he heard the publican call for attention and make his announcement. As a path cleared, he allowed himself to be ushered towards the musicians, amid sporadic trickles of applause. Three songs later, he made his escape to a chorus of *'more, more.'* As the ovation died, he took a deep swallow from his glass and ordered a refill.

"Now, that's more like it." He swung around to find himself face-to-face with the girl from the hotel. "Brenda told me you were a singer but... "

...But I didn't notice how beautiful you were... Christ, he thought, *I'm staring...* The girl's lips had widened to an alluring smile.

"I thought she might have been biased, but... " She added, her eyes twinkling at his confusion.

"Sisters are supposed to be biased." He quipped, praying that he sounded casual. He paid for his drink, his brain struggling for words; the girl saved him the bother.

"So, will we have a sing-song at the hotel later, you have brought your guitar?" Her smile faded at the shake of his head. "Why?"

"Ah, I haven't played in years... I..."

"What about those songs just now? You were great!" He gave her the ghost of a smile, thinking, *it's been a while since anybody described me as great...*

"Thanks. Is there someplace to smoke?"

"Good idea; follow me." She led the way towards the rear exit.

A string of coloured bulbs arcing above a hissing patio heater did little to disguise the austerity of the felt-roofed lean-to. The girl stretched her dark sweater below the hips of her blue denims before easing onto a wooden bench. After a moment's hesitation, he joined her and shielded his lighter towards her cigarette. Briefly, her hands cupped his, until the smoke billowed to her satisfaction. To the backdrop of others' mingled conversations, they smoked in companionable silence until they were suddenly alone.

"I once ruined a brand new pair of trousers here." He muttered.

"Come on, you can't just stop now; spill the gory details."

"It's silly... really. It was the night after we'd got our Leaving Cert results. We were all inside, drinking after-hours, when the guards raided. We ran out here and tried to escape over the back wall. Most of us made it. I ended up tearing a huge hole in the seat of my pants, but the lads who were caught and summoned were only fined a fiver. I was disgusted, I'd just paid fifteen quid for my new *Farah* trousers and they'd been ruined... all for the sake of a bloody fiver!"

"Poetic justice." She chuckled and fished for another cigarette. Silently, he handed her his lighter.

"Are you here on your own?" She ventured, as he finished his cigar.

"Yes, my... I came alone." *Oh no, not more of it!*

"That makes two of us; who wants complications anyway?" She smiled, displaying strong even teeth, the glow from the gas heater smouldering in the dark of her eyes.

"I *am* married, it's just..." He broke off, thinking, *at least, I've set the boundaries.*

"Brenda did say that you might be on your own." Her words were barely audible.

"No, it was very much a last minute decision, I..." *Why am I defending her?*

"I suppose, there's a difference between being married and having a marriage." *You can sing that one*, he thought, but found himself saying.

"Maybe, but let's not forget why we're here!"

"Why are *you* here?"

"I'm here for Brenda's wedding, of course."

"No, I don't mean in town; I mean *here*, in this pub... or yard or whatever!"

"I don't know, maybe I wanted a bolt-hole from the piteous, self-righteous nods of all those model citizens back at the hotel. What's your excuse?"

"Brenda said you'd gone for a walk. Remembering the session, I thought I'd try here."

Jesus, he thought, *she doesn't mess about. How do I get out of this... or... do I really want to...?*" Hands trembling, he lit another cigar.

"I've wanted to meet you for ages." The girl continued, "It's Brenda's fault really, she's always comparing us. *'You sound just like my brother... Only you and my brother would find that funny... What a shame he's married; you'd make a great couple.'* So, I was curious to see for myself what the famous big brother is like. You know how wedding receptions are: so many people, so much small talk... all the family stuff. I mightn't get the chance tomorrow."

"So, what's the verdict?" He asked tentatively, his thoughts molten with possibilities.

"I think you're a-bit-of-all-right!" Her eyes burned into his, her nostrils dilating. "So?"

"So?" He mimicked. She leaned towards him; he met her lips halfway, exploring briefly until approaching voices shattered the spell. She sprang to her feet and flashed him a brief challenging stare before barging her way back indoors.

"What?" She spat, whirling around, as his reaching hand retarded her progress towards the street.

"Wait, let's have a drink."

"Why? I don't want a drink; come on!"

"Hold on, let's just talk for a minute and get a couple of things straight."

"What's there to get straight? Let's go to your..."

"No, not the hotel. There are too many people there; besides, I'm not sure that we..."

"Do you fancy me?" At his nod, she released a long sigh. "Well, what's the problem? We are consenting adults, two lonely people together."

"We don't want any complications; I've got enough..."

"You have nothing to fear from me, I'm not into the *Fatal Attraction* thing. This is all about here and now. We both know there's no future in this so how can there be any complications? Look, I'll cut to the chase: you've got me all worked up but, if you're not game, I'll check out what's still available at the hotel!"

Although her apartment was less than a two-minute walk from the pub, he felt as though they'd been on the street for an age. As she opened her door, he took a furtive backward glance before darting into the hallway. He followed her up the stairs, through the landing, to a compact kitchen/living room.

"Sorry." She said, sweeping a little pile of underwear from the radiator. "I wasn't expecting company." He swallowed hard against the rioting butterflies in his stomach. She indicated the array of spirit bottles on her sideboard.

"No thanks." He managed before her lips found his and, locked in her embrace, he found himself being edged towards the bedroom.

As her fingers tore at his shirt buttons, he eased her sweater over her spiky hair. Her pelvis thrust against him as her breasts popped free from the confinement of her bra.

God, his desire screamed, *I can't remember ever being this turned on. How could I have forgotten how good it feels; how long will it be before I feel this way again? Oh, God.* He rolled sideways, disengaging from her embrace.

"I'm sorry!" He gasped.

"What's wrong?" She asked, half-rising to wriggle free of her jeans.

"The bathroom? I need to..." Self-consciously, his hands dropped to shield his manhood.

"Just there!" She pointed, her relief tinkling around the room.

You can't, you can't. He mouthed to the face in the mirror. *As if things weren't bad enough. Even if she never found out, you'd always know... you'd never forgive yourself.* After running the tap for a moment, he took a deep breath before returning to the bedroom. She was completely naked now, in a classic *reclining nude* pose, her head at a jaunty angle, propped up by her right elbow. Her left hand swung in an exaggerated arc to conjure a condom from the shelf of her locker. Matter-of-factly, she ripped it open with her teeth and, dangling the latex between scarlet thumb and forefinger nails, spat the wrapper at his feet. Transfixed to the spot, he gaped for a moment before finally managing to mumble.

"I am so sorry but this is a mistake. It's not you, you are gorgeous, truly wonderful and I really want to, but..." He fled the bedroom, retrieved his jacket from the hall floor and vanished into the night.

She wasn't in church for the ceremony nor did she appear for the photographs afterwards. It wasn't until everybody had been seated for the meal that he eventually spotted her at a distant table. Once, during his speech, he caught her eye, she nodded slowly, non-judgementally. Afterwards, he danced with the bridesmaids, he danced with the bride; he danced with the groom's mother, her sisters and their daughters and finally, after one last dance with his sister, he gathered his gear from his room and checked out.

She discarded her half-smoked cigarette as he crossed the hotel car park towards her. He marvelled at how natural it seemed: she, half-sitting on the nose of his car, looking resplendent in her cerise cocktail dress. For one fanciful moment, he imagined a weekend-bag at her feet.

What do I say to her, what can I say? Once again she spared him the ordeal.

"You're taking off?" A nod was all he could muster. "Does Brenda know?" He was beside her now, he could smell her perfume, her hair, her...

"Yeah, she understands. Look, I..." She raised a silencing palm.

"Shhh, there's no need, I just wanted to tell you that it's ok. You're a lovely guy, I just hope it works out." She leaned forward, her glossed lips brushing his cheek.

"Thanks, you are one very special lady."

He nodded, as though to add weight to the words. Slowly, she turned; her arms folded against the chill, and took a couple of uncertain high-heeled steps before whirling back to face him.

"Have you got a phone with you?"

"Yes, but..."

"Give it to me."

"What?"

"*Give…it…to…me!*" He obeyed, taking a step towards her; her fingers flew across the keypad.

"If you ever need… want to talk… or… anyway." She slipped the device into the breast pocket of his suit and then, bowing to smell his carnation, gave his arm a gentle squeeze. "Bye." She said simply and started purposefully back towards the function room.

Why, oh why? He asked himself for the umpteenth time. *She'd have never have known, even suspected. Who would ever tell her? Not Brenda; Brenda can't stand her. Nobody would be happier than Brenda if I did happen to meet someone…*

Although night was closing in as he parked behind her car in their driveway, the house was in total darkness. Suddenly concerned, he sprinted up the path and unlocked the hall door. He called her name; there was no response. Flicking light switches as he went, he took the stairs three at a time, only vaguely aware of the familiar items on the hall radiator.

She wouldn't, he reasoned, *she wouldn't harm herself. Yes, the drama would appeal to her but she's not one for accepting consequences. Unless…* On impulse, he pulled open her wardrobe to reveal all of her favourite outfits waiting patiently on their hangers. *I should have known that I'd never be that lucky.* Sighing, he drew the curtains and began to dress the unmade bed. It was then that he noticed the red condom wrapper that had lain hidden beneath the tousled duvet. As his initial mask of shock thawed to an ironic grin, he fished in his jacket for his surviving cigar. After a couple of deep puffs, he opened his phone and, having confirmed that his hotel room was still available, scrolled to the most recent entry in his address book.

LAST DANCE

Drooped heads swung furtively at the sound of steel-tipped shoes tapping up the aisle of the little country chapel. The embroidered capes of the three costumed teenage girls swirled as they spun around before the altar rails to face the congregation. We should have been prepared. After all, had the offertory gifts not included his gold medal from the *Feis* and a framed sepia photograph of the master in youthful artistic glory?

From the choir loft, a fiddler bowed *The Boys of Blue Hill*. As one, three pairs of nimble feet battered out their staccatos on the gleaming black-and-white tiled floor, while bouncing Tara brooches eerily winked reflected candlelight. Their tribute delivered, the dancers genuflected to self-consciously hesitant applause before forming a little triangle at the head and sides of their great-grandfather, as his coffin was wheeled towards the door.

"He'd have enjoyed the send-off." The footballer's hushed words rocked me back to reality.

"That he would." I murmured, taking my place in the procession.

At the graveside, as the priest's monologue undulated to a distant drone, my mind returned to a scene almost two decades past: the senior citizens' party in the village school hall.

After the meal, we had played the obligatory succession of waltzes between the occasional party-piece of a song or recitation from the floor. When, after about three hours, the majority of the guests had been reclaimed by their families, I felt a tug on the sleeve of my pullover. I leaned towards the old man seated opposite me; he whispered conspiratorially in my ear.

"That was great music ye gave us."

"I'm glad you enjoyed it." I smiled; he nodded, applying pressure to my forearm.

"They're nearly all gone now. Is there any chance ye'd play one hornpipe before ye go?" I failed to conceal my surprise.

"A hornpipe?" The effort showed on his leathery features as his chair scraped closer.

"Maybe *The Boys of Blue Hill?*"

"I suppose we could but..."

"Good boy, but leave it for a few more minutes." He lifted his empty glass and eyed me hopefully.

As casually as possible, I reached towards a half-full whiskey bottle. His eyes twinkled as the amber spirit swirled in a little eddy inside his glass.

"Ok?" I prompted.

"Maybe a dropeen of water?" I obliged *"Sláinte, a bhuachaill!"*

"Sláinte is saol!" I acknowledged his toast with my teacup, before relaying his request to my colleagues. *'We will of course...' 'Ah, God help us...' 'Sure we couldn't refuse him.'* I glanced from one nodding head to another.

"Who is he?" My question drew a look of tolerant annoyance from my father.

"Isn't that *The Dancer* himself!" He hissed.

"Oh!" I gasped, my eyes drifting to the pair of heavy blackthorn sticks that lay against the side of the old man's chair.

"I thought about asking him but..." My father continued. "Lads, let ye get ready; *you*, come with me!"

On my father's instructions, I placed a pair of sturdy dining chairs back-to-back, about three-feet apart. The dancer extended his elbows, allowing us to heist him to a position from where he was able to grip the backs of the chairs, thus supporting his bodyweight with his arms. With a tight smile he winked his readiness to my father. Arthritically deformed hands curved, talon-like, around polished wood, while bared dentures made a yellow gash in a weathered mask of ecstatic agony. Myopic eyes blazed with youthful desire, as crippled feet, temporarily released from their lifelong burden, rejoiced, recalled and responded to the tune.

Agape, I marvelled at the incongruity of the spectacle. Braced against the supporting chairs, the mannequinesque rigidity of his arms, head and torso was in eerie contrast to the fluidity of movement below the hips. Each complex manoeuvre was as though choreographed by some great invisible string-pulling hand. I was no dancer but, although I had been privileged to observe some of the very best; I had never seen anything like this. Even the ravages of time and illness were powerless to distort the intricacies of the steps and the genius of the performer.

With a loud *"Hup."* he swung his legs forward and upward before landing to an instant full stop, with all the flourish of an Olympic gymnast. My spontaneous applause was unceremoniously curtailed by the urgency in my father's words.

"Come on, quick; we'd better get him down." Taking an arm each, we eased the breathless figure back to his seat. "By God, you can still do it." My father said, freshening the dancer's glass. The dancer nodded, his bright grin darkening with pain as effort-swollen hands inched trembling feet towards positions of lesser discomfort.

"Sure, 'twas the power of drink that made me chance it." The dancer gasped gamely. As I turned to follow my father, I again felt the pressure on my sleeve. The dancer repeated a series of numbers.

"You might phone my neighbour and tell him I'm ready."

"Sure I'll drive you; I'm passing your door with an empty car." It was a lie but I felt strangely obliged to tender some form of payment for his amazing performance. My offer was accepted and I was soon rekindling the fire in his open hearth, enthralled by stories of a forgotten age.

After that, I became a fairly frequent visitor to his house but I was totally unprepared for his request on one particularly sultry September evening.

"Where will you be watching the All Ireland?"

"I'll be watching it at home, why?"

"Would it be all right if I went in to you?"

"Of course, sure I'll collect you. I'll come early and we'll have a bit of lunch." This was no ordinary All Ireland final. Not only was our own county in action but also, that year's team captain was from our very own parish. After the meal, I switched on the

TV and, while half-heartedly watching the minors of Dublin and Galway, attempted to keep my guest entertained.

"You must have seen the best of them play?" In my experience, men of the dancer's generation invariably rated the heroes of their own era far ahead of the modern pretenders.

"No."

"No? But..."

"I was never at a match..."

"Never?"

"Nor watched one on the box until today. So, you're going to do me the favour of telling no one about this until I'm well dead and gone!"

"If that's what you want..."

"You're a good boy. I knew it that first day at the party... when you got the whiskey for me..." I nodded in silence; inwardly cursing the position I had put myself in. The reason I watched big games at home rather than in the pub was to avoid having to listen to the comments of the disinterested and unenlightened. Now, I had brought one into my home.

The transformation happened the instant our team took to the pitch. The dancer carefully polished his spectacles and craned his neck forward towards the screen.

"That's him." He uttered in a throaty cackle. "By God, 'tis him for sure. He's there all right. Good boy you are..." I blinked against the mist in my eyes, as the boy from out-the-road proudly led his county in step behind the melodious pageantry of the Artane Band. From the moment the ball was thrown in until the half-time whistle, my guest uttered not a single word. Over a hurriedly poured cup of tea, I tried to initiate some form of dialogue but the dancer was not to be distracted from the studio panel's analysis of the game.

As the second half of the match drew to a close and our boys continued to add to their unassailable lead, the county's newest football fan gradually began to relax. At the final whistle, I detected a whispered *"Yes."* but felt it inappropriate to comment. As the victorious captain climbed towards the presentation rostrum, my guest emitted a long sigh and pointedly consulted his pocket watch.

"Good God, is it that time?"

"Do you want to go?"

"Ah sure, whenever you're ready." The sound of his shille-laghs being readied belied the choice suggested in his words.

Feeling strangely cheated at having to miss the after-match TV post mortem, I resolved to force some sort of a comment out of my guest.

"Well, what did you think of the game?" I helped him to his feet.

"I suppose 'twas all right." We shuffled towards the door.

"They won it well." I prompted.

"Ah sure, they were up against nothing." He eased his back-side into the passenger seat and then lifted one leg after the other into position on the floor mat. As I started the engine, my passenger began to whistle a *Ballydesmond* polka, a clear indi-cation that he had no intention of engaging in further conversa-tion. On reaching his home, I broke my five-mile silence.

"Our local man did us proud today." For several moments I feared that he was going to ignore my comment completely. I helped him from the car to the doorstep but only when he had turned the key in the lock, did he finally speak.

"He was the best of them all right, he was the best of them by a long way; what harm but, he had the makings of a fine dancer..."

After the burial, I allowed myself to be swept along with the human tide that flowed determinedly towards the village pub. It was instantly obvious that the elderly licensees had done the dancer proud. The arrival of each mourner was greeted with the compulsory glass of whiskey, sherry or soft drink, relevant to one's sex or age. On rows of tables along the sidewalls, sheets of tinfoil and cling-film were removed to reveal veritable moun-tains of sandwiches, chicken legs and cocktail sausages, which were followed by homemade apple tart and strong tea from a succession of catering-sized pots.

I was about to offer my cup for a final top-up when the footballer's voice sounded again.

"You were very good to him."

"Ah, he was great company."

"No matter. Look at all these people here today; how many of them ever bothered to take him out for a day or even drop in for a chat?"

"I've no idea." I answered truthfully; the dancer had not been given to discussing his neighbours in my company.

"I haven't either but I'd say they were few and far between."

"Did you know him well?" The footballer seemed taken aback by my question.

"I don't suppose I did, although I did go to him for dancing lessons for a while. He was an amazing man, a great teacher. Even though he couldn't leave the chair, he'd still show us the steps by lifting one leg across the other. What I wouldn't give to have seen him actually dance."

While we are all rightly proud of our All Ireland medal winners, there are some of us just can't resist the temptation to get one up on them.

"I saw him dance!" My words struck home; the footballer gaped in incredulity.

"You couldn't have, you're too young!" I related my experience from the Christmas party. "By God, I heard about that; were you there? That was his last dance ever; I'd love to have seen it." A tiny tear glistened in the corner of his eye. Almost regretting my boast, I changed the subject.

"He enjoyed your All Ireland..."

"I should have known that you were taking the piss! He hated football; he didn't talk to me for a couple of years after I packed in the dancing to play with the juveniles."

"Maybe so, but he watched that match with me and, no... he hadn't forgiven you. His only comment afterwards was: *'what harm but, he had the makings of a fine dancer.'* "

"That would be him all right." The footballer smiled wistfully.

"By his judgement, you fell by the wayside."

"Maybe he was right at that!"

"What, and you after captaining your county to All Ireland glory?"

"Tell me this. Would you swap that memory of him dancing between those chairs for any All Ireland final?" I didn't need to answer; we both already knew. For one fanciful moment I thought I could hear a throaty cackle from a stage even higher than the hallowed steps of the Hogan Stand...

CAROL'S CHRISTMAS

After the phone call from Sue, Carol's drive across the city was haunted by images of the twins, not as they were now but as they had been... as toddlers, as growing boys, as teenagers...

John's electronically distorted voice sounded an instant after she pressed the intercom buzzer. His door swung open even as she alighted from the lift.

"So, what's all the fuss about?" John made no attempt to hide his annoyance at his sister's intrusion.

"Yes, I'm fine, thank you for asking, and yes, I do have better things to do on a Friday evening, but I thought that I should tell you in person." Carol pushed the door shut before sinking into the nearest armchair. "Did Mum call?" She used her best big-sister tone.

"Why?" His lower lip protruded sulkily.

"Did you tell her that you'd be there?"

"I left it sort of vague..."

"You said that you would but you've no intention of going, like always."

"I was there last New Year." The lip appeared again.

"It was the one before last!"

"Look, she knows I'm busy. When were you last there?"

"Halloween. Before that, for her birthday in February; I was also there for a few days at Easter and a week in both June and August."

"But you have school holidays, I only get paid when I work..."

"She wants everyone there by the twenty-third. Besides, how many homes do you intend to repossess over Christmas?"

"Everyone? Even the eco warrior?" Carol ignored the reference to their brother.

"Sue thinks that Mum wants to make an announcement; maybe she's selling up."

The camper van appeared on the day the schools closed for the holidays: Friday, December twenty-second. Passing her mother's farmyard, Sue stifled a groan at the sight of the rusting hulk beside the empty hayshed; her offspring were considerably more enthusiastic about the new arrival.

"Uncle Jamie, Uncle Jamie!" Katie and Jack shrieked in unison, squirming free of their rear seat restraints.

"Can we go to Granny May's, Mum, please?" Katie squealed.

"Uncle Jamie, Uncle Jamie!" Jack chanted, his breath blowing ghosts from his lowered window.

"You must change out of your uniforms; then we'll see..." She parked her Zafira and released her brood.

"Please, Mum, please..."

"Uncle Jamie, Uncle Jamie..." The pleas persisted.

Fifteen minutes later, Sue traced her children's steps along the lane to her mother's home. Her progress towards the farmhouse door was abruptly halted by the emergence of a tall brindle hound from within. The animal arched its back and emitted a low growl, its bared teeth, menacing white serrations beneath a shaggy muzzle.

"Down *Gandhi*!" Mother's voice rang out.

"It's *Ganja*, Granny May." Katie corrected but the beast had already got the message and, giving a wide berth to the intruder, flopped onto its belly and crawled beneath the camper.

"Ganja! Ganja!" Jack squealed, ignoring his mother and sprinting towards the animal.

"Sue, just in time." Mother had assumed a sentry-like pose in the doorway. "Can you give Jamie a lift into town?"

"Why?"

"Doesn't the boy deserve a drink after driving all the way from west Cork. I'll keep an eye on these two."

"I wanna go, I wanna go!" Katie squirted out sideways between her grandmother and the doorjamb.

"Me too, me too!" Jack pleaded."

"Ok, come on." Sue sighed, "What's one more child, either way?" Sighing, Sue started the engine, issuing *belt-up* reminders as she steered out of the yard.

"You've got so big, Katie, what age are you now?" Jamie had insisted on sitting in the back seat, between the children.

"I was seven in August, I had a party and all. You didn't..."

"I'm nearly *thickt*, am I getting big too?" Jack lisped through the gap in his milk teeth.

"You're both nearly as big as your mother. Right, Sue? And how's Gary?" Sue took a deep breath before replying.

"It's Barry. You know very..."

"Oh, I know who you married, but how's Gary?" Sue's answer was to bring the car to a sliding halt, a few hundred yards short of Jamie's destination.

"Goodbye, Jamie!" Their eyes locked in her rear-view mirror: hers, smouldering black coals in a deathly wan mask; his, dark pools of innocence in a little island of weathered skin, between encroaching forests of dark hair.

"Goodbye, Uncle Jamie." The children chorused.

"Goodbye... goodbye." Kissing nephew first and then niece, Jamie opened the car door. "Thanks for the lift, Sue. See you later." If there was a response, it was lost against the revving of the engine and the protests of tortured tyres.

When Saturday finally dawned, Sue bowed to the inevitable and allowed the children to go help with Granny May's Christmas decorations. At least, Barry's customary lie-in would give her some breathing space. She needed time: time to think; time to ponder the pros-and-cons of the steps that she might have to take to address her unforeseen dilemma. Maybe she should have invited Jamie to the children's birthday parties. If only last Christmas hadn't happened... if only...

"God, the peace." Sue jumped at Barry's words. "Are the kids at May's?" Her reaction had gone unnoticed. She heard him switch the kettle on.

"They are. Gosh is it that time, do you want some breakfast?" She pinched her cheeks and turned towards the kitchen.

"You're ok," she almost gasped at the reprieve, "I'm due in town, I'll get something there."

Barry and Carol met at the junction of their lane with the main road; they both slowed and lowered their windows.

"The kids are at your mother's; it's just Sue at home."

Am I that transparent? Carol wanted to ask, but merely smiled and said:

"Thanks, I'll see you later." Already, through the crisp distance, she could hear the children's excited calls. For an instant something gnawed deep within her, but only for an instant. Approaching the farm entrance, she slowed to a crawl. From the open gateway, a pair of sombre little figures waved politely. *Ho, bloody ho!* She thought, returning their waves and then screamed as a huge shaggy monster gaped through her open window. Instinctively, she accelerated towards safety and Sue, all too aware of the whoops of glee and barks of triumph that her undignified departure had generated.

Sue was already on the threshold but, instead of the dreaded claustrophobic sisterly hug, Carol found herself being gently, but firmly, eased away from the door.

"No," Sue was saying, "don't go in."

"But I need a coffee." Carol protested.

"Fine, go ahead and make a coffee, make two coffees but first give me a bloody cigarette."

"Yes, it's lovely to see you too and my journey was..." Something in Sue's expression caused Carol to stop in mid-sentence. "Two sugars?" Carol confirmed before surrendered her cigarettes and lighter.

Sue seemed calmer when Carol emerged from the house.

"It's Jamie!" Sue sighed, emitting a cloud of smoke.

"It's always Jamie!" Carol agreed neutrally, placing the coffees on the windowsill before selecting a cigarette. "The... children like him, but I suppose he can relate to their level." She lit her cigarette. "Is it the camper?"

"The camper?" Sue eyed the butt of her cigarette distastefully before carefully concealing it beneath a handful of chippings at the edge of the driveway.

141

"You know, lowering the tone of the neighbourhood and all that. That *is* why you opposed his planning application last year?"

"Carol, would you want a field full of *Jamies* camped next-door to you?" Sue lit another cigarette. "No, it's not about the camper; it's worse." She took a long drag and exhaled. "It's about Katie!"

Jamie was still the subject when Carol reached her mother's house.

"You've just missed Jamie." May eyed her daughter from above her rimless reading glasses. "Katie said that you'd passed down." May brushed a stray wisp of brown-tinted hair from her brow and smiled, recalling the child's actual words: *'The dragon lady is gone to our house.'*

"Where is Jamie; in the pub, I suppose?" She removed her jacket and flopped into an armchair.

"No, he wouldn't drink and drive; he had to meet someone on business." Carol allowed herself a tight smile but refrained from commenting. "He brought a turkey and a ham – both free range – and a tree that's still growing in a bucket."

And probably stolen. Carol mentally added. Unlike her siblings, Carol had no real problem with Jamie's preferred position in their mother's affections and the fact that he had *business* in town meant one of two positives: either he was selling, and would be able to buy his round in the pub, or he was buying, which meant a fresh stash to ease a big sister through the trials of a family Christmas.

John also had business in town. After a perfunctory handshake, he got straight to the point.

"How much?"

"Seventy-five." Barry answered, placing a *cappuccino* before his brother-in-law.

"He was more than fair with you. Does anyone else know?" Barry's dark curls shook briefly. "Good, how much do you need?" Barry exhaled through compressed lips before replying.

"I could cope with forty-five but a bit more would make things easier."

"Fifty-five? Or, we could probably do sixty at a push."

"Fifty-five is perfect. Thanks, John, I'd better go. He'll be waiting." They shook again and Barry took his leave, his right fist clenched in triumph. *One down, one to go.*

The rattling of Jamie's approaching wagon sent Carol hurrying from the kitchen.

"I just need a quick word with him... in private, Mother!" The addendum stopped May in her tracks.

"The dog goes; you stay!" Carol hissed as the grumbling engine finally silenced.

"The dog stays; we walk!" Jamie scratched the lurcher's chin before closing the door of the vehicle and starting back towards the main road on foot. "Well, what have I done now?"

"Katy!"

"Katy?" Jamie's surprise seemed genuine.

"Sue just told me everything. You shouldn't have thrown that in her face."

"Ah, the Gary thing! Sue shouldn't have objected to my planning application, it wasn't as if I was looking for the whole bloody farm."

"Still, that was low..."

"Oh, so that's how it is! Look, Carol, everyone has a go at me; Jamie-bashing is what keeps this family together. I know you're not the worst of them, but even you've had your moments."

"Jamie, listen..."

"No, *you* listen. Ok, I admit I was wrong but... all that moral high-ground crap just got to me. The good news is that things have changed... I promise you now that I'll never hop that ball again."

If any resentment remained after they'd shared a joint, it quickly evaporated when John's black BMW swung into the lane. As one, they withdrew to the safety of the grass margin, their right hands raised in brief acknowledgement of their brother's curt nod.

"Wouldn't I love to be Katie's position?" Jamie's words were hushed, as if meant only for his own ears.

"How unlucky was that? And she to bump into you, of all people."

"Of all the bars in all the towns, they had to end up at our session. *Honeymoon baby*, my foot. I wonder how many more hen-party babies are running around the place?"

"But you'd never know: except for her blue eyes, Katie and Jack could pass as twins!"

"Like John and me?"

"But seriously, Jamie; you will have to talk to Sue." She mirrored Jamie's grin.

"Consider it done!"

May made her announcement as Carol began to clear the dinner dishes.

"I'm babysitting Sue's two tonight and Jamie has arranged for a cab to take the rest of you into town. Enjoy it, because tomorrow night, I want you all here, sober and on your best behaviour. Now buzz off and get ready; you too, Carol, I'll finish up here."

Even after two stiff gins-and-tonics, Carol sat in silent awe of the incongruous normality of the scene around her. Not only were Sue and Jamie talking, they were virtually inseparable: their heads unhealthily close, their bodies jerking with hushed conspiratorial laughter. Barry and John were also hitting it off, apparently in total agreement with each other's entrenched points of view. Despite her many encounters with old friends and acquaintances and, the occasional admiring glance from a new face, Carol found herself pining for the familiar tensions of Christmases past.

About a half-hour later, Carol's evening reached a new high when she met David in the smoking area.

"Carol." David finally managed. "You're looking great, a happy Christmas to you."

"And to you and yours. How is everyone?" She declined his proffered cigarette but accepted his light for one from her own stock.

"Oh, good, thanks, good... good!"

"Good!" She nodded, little jets of smoke spurting from her nostrils.

"Well, actually, we've separated..."

"Oh." Both cigarettes glowed briefly. "I'm sorry. It must be tough... especially at Christmas... I mean... the kids..." She added lamely.

"Oh, I'll be there for Christmas – for the dinner anyway. I'm staying with Dad at present." They both turned as their moment was shattered by the noisy arrival of Jamie and Sue. "I'll see you, Carol, take care."

"Yes, you too David." She watched him walk past the pub's rear entrance, onto the street, where he turned left and disappeared without a backward glance.

The surreal calm continued throughout Christmas Eve morning. Returning from some last minute shopping, Carol was greeted by the unlikely sight of her twin brothers and Jamie's mongrel heading towards the sheep path that led to the highest point of the farm. On impulse, she drove to Sue's house and rang the doorbell. Failing to get a response, she rang again and then, after a pause, rang a third time.

"Jesus, what's the panic?" Sue appeared in her dressing gown, looking flushed, almost glowing. "I thought it was Granny Joan bringing the kids back."

"I need to borrow your wellies..."

"In the garage!" Sue's door slammed shut.

The twins sat side-by-side, their backs to her, on a dry-stone wall at the brow of the hill.

"...Stephen's morning." John sounded almost apologetic. From the cover of a clump of gorse bushes, Carol made the most of the rare opportunity to eavesdrop on her brothers.

"What's your hurry, have you found a new boyfriend or something?"

Shit, Jamie! Carol's hand dropped to cover her mouth but then rose to shield her eyes against the low winter sun.

"Actually, I have, but keep it to yourself." Carol gaped in awe as the brothers spontaneously embraced, their hands slapping each other's shoulders. Carol glanced skyward, mouthing rare words of thanks.

The dinner table was laid when Jamie finally emerged – hair and beard still glistening – after his shower. He surprised everyone by taking a teaspoon and clinking it against a wine glass.

"Thank you." He said huskily, as four pairs of eyes bore into him. "Don't worry, I'm not going to make a speech but my little sister has a bit of news that concerns you all. Sue?" She needed no second bidding.

"Thank you, Jamie. There is something that I'd like to say to all of you. Thanks! Thank you, Mother, for all of us being here… Thank you, Carol, for your wisdom, for your advice and… and for being my sister. Thank you, John, for making it possible for us to buy Jamie's site. Thank you, Jamie, for being a bigger person than me."

"Holy God, hold on one minute." May leapt from the table and rummaged briefly in the dresser drawers before returning to place a candle in the centre of the table.

"Is that a *Millennium Candle*?" Carol finally ventured.

"We didn't light it back then because your father was so poorly, but now I think it's time for new beginnings. Sue, will you do the honours?"

Next morning, to add to the air of incredulity, John volunteered to assist Jamie with the preparation of Christmas dinner. Carol paused from her table-laying duties only to be pressed back into service by May.

"Can you bring that other chair from the scullery?"

"We already have eight places: six adults and two kids…"

"I haven't time to explain now. Just get that chair and then have a drink or a… smoke or… something." Realising the futility of further resistance, Carol complied and then watched while May prepared identical miniature settings at the foot of the table. It wasn't until Sue's gang arrived that Carol finally went outside for a smoke, just as Paddy, their nearest neighbour, parked his Jeep between her Focus and May's Fiesta.

"Carol, happy Christmas to you, girl." David's father nervously swapped a wrapped bottle between his hands.

"Many happy returns, Paddy... Are you going in?" She finally asked.

"Ah, whenever you're ready... take your time." She took a long final drag and discarded her cigarette.

"I'm ready." She strode towards the door thinking, *at last, some excitement.*

Once in the kitchen, Carol slipped onto the nearest chair.

"You all know Paddy." May announced, motioning the new arrival to her side. That's why I wanted you all here today. Paddy has asked me to marry him and I've accepted; whoever wants to attend had better keep Valentine's Day free." Jamie was the first to break the stunned silence and led the congratulatory procession towards the happy couple.

Shortly after Sue's clan had left to visit Barry's parents, Carol emerged from the sanctuary of her bedroom, as John's hushed tones drifted from the parlour.

"You put dope in the giblet soup?"

"When I admitted it to Mother afterwards, she went ballistic but when I pointed out the effect it had on the lot of you, she insisted that I put another bit in the stuffing today." Jamie spluttered.

"But the kids... and poor Paddy?" John sounded quite breathless.

"The kids don't eat stuffing... and Paddy seemed happy enough..."

In the living room, May and Paddy snored in tandem from twin armchairs at either end of *Ganja,* who lay sprawled before the glowing turf fire. Carol crept to the kitchen and, donning May's anorak, slipped a wedge of iced cake and a bottle of wine into the pockets.

The lane stretched invitingly before her, its frozen verges glistening in an almost full moon. Reaching Paddy's yard, she paused to admire the reflection of the house's festive lights in the windscreen of David's dark Volvo estate. Sitting on the warm bonnet of the car, she lit a cigarette and smoked it through before advancing to tap rhythmically on the sitting room window.

147

JUST THE JOB

It was one of those days when grey was more than just a colour. Leaden clouds, indistinguishable from a haze of streets, buildings and roofs, crowded dissolute faces and dreary suits towards the ineluctability of evening city gridlock. Even the distant green traffic lights seemed unusually anaemic, only their amber and red companions added intermittent hints of lustre to the gloomy vista. The only light at the end of this particular tunnel was that which prolonged Hogan's entombment in an opaque veil of nothingness. It was as if autumn had breathed its last and succumbed to the all-consuming inevitability of winter.

Yes, Hogan mused, drumming a steering wheel accompaniment to the frantic swishing of his wipers. *If the sky is ever going to fall, this could well be the day.*

Seventy minutes later, Hogan left the glaring frenzy of the motorway for the muted obscurity of a moonless rural night. He was now in alien territory, totally reliant on his sat-nav to guide him through the maze of secondary roads that crisscrossed the midland counties.

Illuminated in the Saab's headlights, mile after mile of hawthorn hedging undulated by. Except for haphazard splashes of dark parasitic ivy, the leafless tangle of entwined branches was a solid grey-brown wall: that nondescript monochrome of old plasticine after its original rainbow colours have been rolled together.

Every now and then, the monotony was broken when little verdant oases of conifers or other evergreens hinted at human habitation. Occasionally, his spirits rose when the glow of an oncoming vehicle reassured him that he wasn't completely alone; sometimes, he dimmed and slowed in silent wonder when an unidentifiable flash of saturated fur melted back into the void.

When he finally reached the hotel car park, Hogan reversed into the space beside a green Land Rover, which was parked precisely as Gallagher had predicted. Taking a powerful torch from the Saab, Hogan boarded the unlocked Land Rover; a quick rummage in the glove box yielded the vehicle's key and the biro-drawn map that would lead him to his ultimate goal.

The downpour had almost ceased when, ten minutes later, Hogan paused beside a pair of crumbling entrance piers. After consulting his map, he steered the 4x4 from the road to rattle downhill along a rough tree-lined track. Wrestling the wheel, Hogan swore at each protruding branch that flailed against the windscreen, his ears alive to the constant swishing of dying bracken against the underside of the vehicle.

Soon, the features of a deserted farmyard materialised out of the gloom. The jeep's full headlights outlined the rusting ribs of a roofless barn, now listing at a gravity-defying angle towards the naked weathered timbers of a series of stone outbuildings. Hogan swung the jeep in a wide arc that brought him to the rear of an unlit dwelling house. Killing both engine and lights, he took his torch and waded through the waves of ragwort, thistle and dock that washed against his thighs. At his approach, a sudden squall creaked a lopsided door inward.

With the aid of his torch, Hogan located the stairway and proceeded cautiously towards the faint outline of a landing window. A quick glance through the chilly expanse confirmed Gallagher's assessment. Suppressing a shudder, he emitted a long sigh before retracing his steps back to the jeep.

The vehicle count in the hotel car park had almost doubled during Hogan's absence. Having parked the jeep facing towards the exit gate, he retrieved his overnight bag and an aluminium briefcase from the boot of his car and entered the hotel.

A cursory glance told Hogan that the night's accommodation would fall someway short of what Gallagher provided for his city assignments. In the foyer, a little scattering of ghoulish Halloween decorations seemed eerily at home against the Gothic backdrop of high oak-beamed ceilings, bare limestone walls and partially carpeted floorboards. His *en-suite* room was basic in the extreme: a four-foot bed, a pair of mismatched lockers, a free-standing wardrobe, a tiny dressing table and a pair of rickety chairs.

"It's just for one night." Gallagher had promised *"In, out and away."* The words resonated in Hogan's mind as, after prevailing against his temperamental shower, he changed into a blue woollen sweater and a pair of navy slacks. Feeling renewed, he followed his nose towards the appetising aroma that wafted up from the ground floor.

Accustomed to the pretentiousness of Dublin menus, Hogan almost cheered at the sight of a mixed grill among that evening's specials. Once his hunger had been sated, he decided to enjoy his paper and coffee in the comfort of a fireside armchair in the residents' lounge.

It was the jangle of his mobile phone that eventually broke Hogan's concentration from his crossword. Placing his newspaper on an adjacent table, he thumbed a response to Gallagher's text message, unaware of the blonde haired woman who had recently sat across from him.

"I can see your problem from here!" Her blue eyes twinkled from above a slim-jim glass. She sampled her colourless drink and, with a swirl of lemon and a tinkling of ice cubes, placed it beside his paper.

"Pardon?" He gasped, gaping at the striking forty-something before him.

"I'm not usually this forward but you are sitting in my favourite chair. It's seventeen across: *weapon*. You've got *firearm* but it should be *shotgun*... because eleven down is *moody*... the *y* fits with *yearn*: twenty-three across... the clue is *long for*... By the way, I'm Marie..." She retrieved her glass and took a lady-like sip.

"Well, thank you, Marie, but I beg to differ..." He retrieved the newspaper. "The clue for eleven down is *grumpy*, but the solution is *surly*, not *moody*. That still fits with *yearn*... but... makes nine across: *speeding*, therefore twelve down is *demand*, so your *shotgun* becomes *firearm*."

"I'm impressed... am... I didn't catch your name..."

"Look, I'm sorry I sat on your chair, but..." He began to fold his newspaper.

"*Joe*, I'll call you *Joe*; you look like a Joe. Have you got a light?" Bemused, he fished a disposable lighter from his back pocket and then grimaced when she leaned across him to light the candle inside the hollowed pumpkin on the stone mantelpiece.

"There." She smiled; admiring her handiwork, then waved the lighter. "Can I borrow this... while I go outside for a cigarette?"

"Keep it." He arose and, gathering his belongings, started towards the lobby. After collecting his key, he returned to his room, stuffed his newspaper into his holdall and, after a moment's indecision, retraced his steps back downstairs.

Marie made no comment when Hogan joined her beneath the Perspex awning at the hotel's rear entrance. As she returned his lighter, a cascade of distant fireworks formed an expanding halo behind her shoulder-length hair. Oblivious to his admiring gaze, she turned back towards the car park.

"Which one is yours?" She finally asked, against a faint staccato of festive bangers.

"Which what?" He took a half step towards her.

"Which van? Judging from your hands, I doubt if you're in the plumbing or drain service business, neither can I see you steel-fixing or fitting PVC windows... Maybe you're one of those *black-hole cowboys*, perhaps the Land...?"

"Over there... by the gate." He lit a cigarette, using the moment to survey the furthermost line of vehicles "It's the red Volkswagen Caddy."

"*1-2-1 Solutions?* It sounds like an answer to a prayer. So, tell me, Joe, what solutions do you offer?" Her cigarette glowed again.

"Are you into I T... computers?" At her grimace, he began to breathe again.

"Oh no... give me the football off-side rule any day..." She took a final drag and flicked the butt away "Will I see you inside?"

"Yeah, in a minute." *Shit!* He thought as she swept back indoors. *What am I at?* Drawing deeply on his cigarette, he renewed the battle with his conscience.

The result was still in the balance when Hogan returned to the lounge.

"Is there a *mister* Marie?" He asked, sitting beside her.

"Yes, but he isn't exactly *my* 1-2-1 solution."

"Doesn't he mind your being here?"

"No, he's away a lot, but tonight he'll be at home, oiling his gun for the morning; he won't even notice that I'm not there."

"The morning?"

"The first of November, the opening of the pheasant season, the only anniversary he ever remembers!"

"I'm sorry. Do you spend much time here? I mean... I shouldn't..."

"Most Tuesdays and the odd Thursday... it depends. I avoid Wednesdays – that's bridge night – and the weekends... when the locals invade."

"He doesn't get suspicious?"

"I do some voluntary work with *The Samaritans*; he'll assume that I'm there."

"What if he phones you?"

"Even if he did, he'd call my mobile... not *their* number."

"But why... why here?"

"Joe, you've seen the car park. For every van out there, there's a man in here... a lonely bored man. I know a lot of women who'd kill for a set-up like this."

Rendered speechless, Hogan readdressed his crossword. Marie tried a new angle.

"I've heard that people who do crosswords have blanks in their lives. Have you got a family, Joe?" She caught him off-guard, as did the promptness of his reply.

"Two: a girl of twenty-six and a boy of twenty-three. I'm divorced!"

"Do you see them?"

"Oh, yes... frequently... Have you...?"

"No... No, I'm glad you mentioned the girl first, most men would say *'a boy and a girl'*, regardless of their ages." She said, watching the pride swell in his eyes.

"Most men don't have a daughter like mine: she's a chartered accountant but her real passion is repairing and racing motorbikes. My son is an architecture graduate but he's presently negotiating a full-time rugby contract."

"Wow, I'm impressed all over again. But what about you, Joe? What do you get up to when you're not doing your one-to-one solutions?" Now there was a question, a very good question and one that Hogan was finding increasingly difficult to ignore.

During his army career, there had never been enough hours in the day; nowadays, his calendar lacked the structure required to actually live a life. Oh, he had money; a lot of money – Gallagher was an industrious agent – and he had time... weeks, sometimes months, between jobs... But anonymity was the name of his game, and his adherence to its rules was such that there were times when even he forgot who he actually was. Tonight he was *Joe*: fifty-something, short, stout and balding Joe; a featureless little man, scuttling all over the country in his red VW Caddy van, to execute his *1-2-1 Solutions* in person.

Christ. Hogan thought. *This is too close to the bone.*

"Joe... *Joe!*" Her words seemed to come from afar. "What now, Joe?"

"Now?" He glanced at his watch.

"Yes." She hissed. "Time and tide, Joe. Is this going somewhere? Because..."

"It's only a little bed..." It was almost an apology.

"I know, I've seen your key but, right now, I'd prefer to be in that little bed with you than in a four-poster with anybody else.

It's been too long... far too long... Hogan thought as Marie's perfume enveloped his senses. Fingers, lips, tongues exploring... demanding, she climbed astride and sank onto him. She moaned softly, her movements carefully measured... then, almost imperceptibly, increasing in intensity, in insistency... Ever

more erratically, her warm breath roared against his eardrum...
He heard her gasp.

No, oh nooo... His brain pleaded. He felt her shudder, felt
her fingernails scythe through the soft flesh of his buttocks. Re-
leasing a long sigh, she rolled onto her back. He turned towards
her, his eyes ablaze with questions.

"Shush..." Marie breathed, her fingers brushing his thighs.
She was kissing him again. His lips, his chin, his throat, his
chest, his navel...

"Are you leaving?" He muttered, shielding his eyes against
the glare through the open bathroom door. Silhouetted between
the jambs, she finished towelling her hair before replying.

"It's all right for you but I've got to go home, go to bed and
get up again, in time to prepare a full Irish breakfast for the
great white hunter. One can hardly expect a member of *Seanad
Éireann* to face a hard day's shooting with just his fasting spit."
She dressed in silence, sitting back on the edge of the bed to
wriggle into her shoes. "Goodbye, Joe..." She leaned sideways
and oozed a slow kiss onto his lips. "You're a good guy, Joe... a
perfect 1-2-1 solution."

"Take care, Marie." He sighed, reaching for a cigarette.

Seanad Éireann? Sweet Jesus, surely it couldn't be?

About four hours later, the reminder tone of Hogan's phone
dissolved the soft warmth of Marie's body from his dreams. A
quick glance through his window confirmed that, although it
wasn't yet quite six-thirty, the car park gates were open – another point to Gallagher. After pulling on a black windcheater
over his navy boiler suit, Hogan donned a pair of thick woollen
stockings and then tied his weatherproof boots. After a final
check on the contents of his briefcase, he listened intently for
several moments before slipping silently into the corridor.

Passing reception, he could hear the hotel stirring to life.
Hardly daring to breathe, he cat-footed his way through the
shuttered residents' lounge and pushed the release bar of the
fire-exit door that led to the car park. Unlocking the Land Rover, he slipped it into neutral, allowing it to freewheel into the
lane, before finally starting the engine.

In the absence of wind and rain, the farmyard seemed even more desolate than before. The only sound was the startled protest of a disturbed barn owl from somewhere in the blackness overhead. Deciding against a torch, he began his ascent, of the stairs, the aura of dank decay intensifying with each cautious step. Once in position, his practised fingers clicked the combination locks open and set to work on the familiar contents of the case.

Once the jigsaw of pieces was assembled and checked, Hogan thrust his surgically gloved hands deep into the pockets of his boiler suit, in a vain effort to evade the numbing chill of the unglazed window. After about twenty minutes, a solitary light appeared in the distance; soon afterwards, another glowed in very close proximity to the first. Only seconds had elapsed before a third, brighter light, flickered to life beneath the others...

Hogan could now distinguish the outline of a large Edwardian house, a dark shape against the paling eastern skyline. It was a full fifty minutes before his eyes detected movement. So well was the figure camouflaged that only a series of ghostly breaths betrayed its approach through the faint morning light. Abruptly, a two-tone spaniel appeared, running in little tight circles around its master, eager to begin the hunt.

Hogan's military trained eye swept the landscape that awaited the pair... there was a double ditch at the end of the next field...no more than a couple of hundred meters from his vantage point... perhaps... He adjusted the *Bausch&Lomb* telescopic scope, fraction by torturous fraction, until he was finally satisfied with the focus. It took another seven minutes for man and dog to reach the boundary. The animal crossed first, splashing through the swollen ditch and clambering up the centre mound, before vanishing again beneath a tail-spray of cascading droplets.

Hogan took a long breath and re-cushioned the fibreglass stock of the weapon against his shoulder. He watched his quarry clear the first channel with an athletic bound and begin to scale the dyke. The man's aristocratic nose was now between the crosshairs of Hogan's sights. Hogan edged the barrel slightly to the right, to a point between the target's left cheekbone and the band of his pheasant-plumed hat.

Exhaling slowly, Hogan squeezed the trigger. The *XM25 US Army* sniper rifle bucked once, the lethal.*308 Winchester* round going straight through its victim before embedding itself somewhere further along the bank. The man collapsed like a rag doll, a finger spasm triggering the shotgun to discharge its load into the popped-up head of the enquiring spaniel.

Watching the body roll into the drain, Hogan felt no elation. In seconds, he disassembled the rifle, restoring each segment to its niche, before stashing the case beneath the passenger seat of the Land Rover. As he drove back towards the road, he was absently aware of haphazard volleys of distant shotgun fire.

A little over an hour later, showered, breakfasted and checked out, Hogan nodded his satisfaction at the absence of the Land Rover from the car park. Passing the red Caddy van, he grinned on reading the small lettering beneath the boldly printed *1-2-1 Solutions*: *Pest Control Services*.

Heading north out of town, he switched his radio on and idly wondered how long it would take for news of his latest solution to hit the airwaves. Absently, his eyes softened at the memory of Marie's parting kiss.

'*You're a good guy, Joe...*' Her words came floating back. Nodding silently, he decided that she'd got it right. He was a good guy... it was just... just the job...

GOOSEBERRY SEASON

It wasn't as if it had been Tommy's first trip over Coom Beama, he had been making the journey – several times a year – for as long as he could remember. This time, however, he wasn't dressed in his Sunday best; this time, he was wearing his after-school run-arounds, while his good clothes, clean underwear and socks were stashed in the battered suitcase in the boot of his mother's car.

There were other items there too, some of which had been bought that very morning with Tommy's child benefit money: a yellow windcheater, a couple of pairs of jeans and a half-dozen coloured tee-shirts. Tommy had greeted these additions to his wardrobe with stoic resignation but it was the morning's final purchase that had set the alarm bells ringing in his brain... the pair of black wellingtons that sat ominously on the back seat beside him.

As usual, on the descent from the pass, the first recognisable landmark was the gable of the squat farmhouse, nestled into the foothills of Slieveduff, on the far side of the valley. The family farm was a living tribute to the resilience of Tommy's ancestors, who had wrestled the prized acres from the relentless bracken, briar and gorse that stalked it from every side. Joe and Eileen now continued the struggle and the walled patchwork of fertile fields bore enduring testament to their labours.

Tommy could picture the scene in the kitchen: Joe, freshly shaven, craning his neck like a love-struck gander against the alien restrictions of collar and tie; Eileen, in a print cotton frock, fingering the new waves in her auburn-tinted hair. Today, however, these images failed to spring the customary flood of anticipation; today, Tommy and his mother would not be returning home with a dozen free-range eggs, a flitch of home-cured bacon or even a box of fresh vegetables; today, Tommy would not be going home at all.

Tommy wasn't your average ten-year-old; he wasn't given to haranguing his mother with an endless stream of unanswerable questions. Tommy was more a listener than a talker and had become quite adept at decoding the obscure nuances of adult conversation. Apparently, Mum *needed a bit of space...time to think...to adjust.*

Last summer, Liam Buckley's mother had suffered those very symptoms, Liam and his little sister had been sent to their grandparents for a fortnight, only to return home and discover that they had gained a pair of baby sisters. Tommy wondered whether his mother would be getting a girl or a boy, he didn't really have a preference... he just prayed that it would be only *one.*

The lake crept into view, its gentle ripples sparkling in the midday sun. For years, Tommy had dreamt of fishing the lake... some people even went out in little bobbing boats... sitting, still figures that only ever moved when an arm would revolve above a shoulder to redirect the fly-cast towards a more likely spot.

Skirting the lake, Tommy could distinguish individual stones on the lake floor: algae-clad shapes, shimmering green beneath the transparent surface. If this dry spell were to continue for much longer, the water level would drop even further, leaving these fragile emerald jackets to shrivel and dry to brittle threads on the expanding shoreline. As they crossed the limestone bridge, their progress was monitored by the calm dark eyes of ruminating cattle that had chosen the comparative cool of the riverbed over the heat of the open pasture.

They were climbing again, passing the derelict schoolhouse where the enthusiasm of nesting swallows had long replaced the reluctance of their human predecessors. This was Tommy's favourite part of the journey; this was where the canine wing of neighbourhood watch came into its own.

As ever, Nan Ryan's pair of Yorkshire terriers formed the vanguard, their excited yapping a rallying call for their cousins from the three homesteads further up the cul-de-sac. Within seconds, sentries appeared at each entrance gate: Molly Donovan's ageing setter with his distinctive sway-back gait, his white muzzle jerking upward with each hoarse bark; Ger McCarthy's Alsatian, a latent threat, sitting resolutely in the centre of the road, his huge radar ears pricked forward towards the trespassers, unflinching as the familiar dark shape of Lass, Uncle Joe's border collie, belly-crawled through the overgrown margin at her side of the road.

Tommy's relationship with Lass had always been one of mutual mistrust. From some hidden vantage point, her keen eyes would monitor his every move until he would unwittingly wander within striking range of her sharp white teeth. Lass was a sneak, a coward; at least, you knew where you were with McCarthy's Alsatian, he would face you, teeth bared in a warning snarl; with him, you would always get a chance to run away...

Mum swerved around the big dog. Tommy pressed his face against the glass of the car window... scarcely a foot away from the animal's lolling tongue; this was the closest he had ever been to the creature, the closest he ever wanted to be. The huge head hung slightly askew, nostrils twitching, as the car swung back to the middle of the road.

The terriers' yapping was receding now. Satisfied that they had driven the intruders from their territory, they strutted back to claim their customary spot on the cottage doorstep. Lass was now running parallel to the car, her pointed muzzle sniping at the revolving tyres. As usual, she refrained from giving tongue until the car had actually entered the farmyard. At Joe's snarled command, the collie ceased her racket and slunk sullenly towards the empty hayshed at the far end of the yard.

Surprisingly, Joe was not clad in his Sunday best: a colourless shirt hung loosely about him and he was barefoot beneath a pair of soiled brown trousers. Eileen, attired in a pale blue housecoat, appeared at the doorway, a flour-powdered tea towel clenched between her red bony fingers. The women exchanged muted greetings as Joe retrieved Tommy's belongings from the car and disappeared indoors. Eventually, it was Eileen who seemed to notice the boy but, instead of inviting him inside or marvelling at how much he had grown, she dismissed him with a backhand wave and told him to go and play with the dog.

After about twenty minutes of defensive manoeuvring, Tommy's ostracism was finally ended when Joe called his name from the threshold. In the kitchen, Mum was already saying her farewells. She placed her open hands briefly on Tommy's shoulders and assured him that he would have a wonderful holiday. After planting a fleeting butterfly peck on her son's cheek, she was gone. Still waving towards the departing vehicle, Tommy found himself being firmly ushered to the kitchen table where Eileen had buttered a plate of warm fruit scones.

By now, Joe was booted and capped and, with a quizzical glance in the boy's direction, escaped to his outdoor domain. Having toyed with his food for some minutes, Tommy was summoned to the little loft room above the kitchen to help Eileen dress the iron-framed single bed where he would sleep for the duration of his stay. How long that stay would be, he didn't know and, judging from the tight-lipped demeanour of his elders, there was little hope of enlightenment anytime soon.

Before Eileen returned downstairs, she indicated the tiny cupboard below the gable window. She referred to it as *Joe's glory hole* and hinted that it might hold something of interest to the boy. Tommy nodded his thanks but, instead of exploring the cobwebbed depths, he elected to sit on the edge of the bed and train his eyes back towards the pass that stood resolutely between him and home.

It was then Tommy realised why he hadn't been allowed to bring his bike. Mum had claimed that there hadn't been room in the car, yet the bike had easily fitted on the back seat only eighteen months before. Yes, it all made sense: with his bike, Tommy would have been able to go home... but Tommy suspected that, right now, home was the place where he would receive the least welcome of all.

Then he saw it... there was no mistaking Mum's green *Fiesta*, labouring up the slope beyond the bridge. Something must have happened to delay her: she should have been well clear of the pass by now... At supper he broached the question with his elders. Crossing herself, Eileen threw her eyes towards the ceiling, while Joe suggested that she might have stopped to chat with a neighbour. Shortly afterwards, even though it was still as bright as day, Eileen pointed authoritatively towards the stairs.

As shadows lengthened across the valley, each flash of re-flected sunshine from the pass brought renewed hope until the approaching vehicle would vanish without trace into the bow-els of the valley below. The night crept gradually in, bringing with it a degree of darkness hitherto unknown to Tommy. How he missed the friendly amber streetlights outside his own bed-room window, it never got this dark back home; it never got this quiet...

Joe's voice sounded from the kitchen.

"And what if she did itself? She knows what..." Eileen's shrieked intervention made it impossible to distinguish the words of either protagonist.

Joe was shouting.

"It's their right..." But again Eileen confused the exchange until Joe's power eventually prevailed.

"The child shouldn't be deprived..." The rest of the sentence was lost against the grating of chair legs against flagstones.

"He'll never turn a key in this door." Eileen screamed as a door slammed and the night fell silent except for the distant plaintive calls of lonely animals.

After breakfast, Joe had a proposition for Tommy.

"Do you fancy a stroll up the mountain today?" Joe licked the final traces of boiled duck egg from his spoon.

"I dunno, I suppose, what...?" It took Tommy a moment to get over the shock of being addressed directly.

"Just for a couple of hours... to have a look at the sheep." It was almost a plea.

"Ok, so. What will I wear?" Tommy asked as Joe lifted his green waxed jacket from its hook on the back door.

"You'll have to dirty those wellingtons sometime... and wear your jacket... there's a different climate on the mountain."

Tommy's enthusiasm for the excursion received a severe blow when Joe whistled for the collie.

"Is she coming too?" The boy pouted, half-turning back to-wards the house.

"There wouldn't be much point in going without her, 'tis on days like this that she earns her keep, it's what she's bred for." Joe stooped to greet the collie.

"I don't want to go." His eyes fixed on the dog; Tommy took a backward step.

"Ah, Tommy." Joe cajoled. "I know you're afraid of her, but this is your chance to get to know her properly. She just doesn't know what to make of you, she can't figure out where you fit in. Look, I'll keep her on a lead until we get to the mountain. Come on!" Joe urged, securing a length of bailing twine around the collie's neck.

What followed was probably the most interesting day of Tommy's young life. As they walked, Joe's descriptive mono- logue metamorphosed the most mundane of weeds and bugs to the most magical of flora and fauna. So engrossing was each new experience that Tommy soon became oblivious to Lass's presence. He needn't have worried; the collie too had been trans- formed. She now pranced along at Joe's side, eyes alert, ears erect, her pink tongue dangling and her feathery tail primed to launch her into action at the merest hint from her master.

At the end of the farm's top meadow, Joe released the collie and waved her forward with a swinging loop of his right arm. Mesmerised, Tommy watched as Lass charged off in a wide arc to disappear behind a screen of gorse, intermittently reappear- ing as a diminishing ant-like speck that inched ever closer to the summit.

"We'll give her time to do the lift but when she comes back with the sheep, I'll let you work her... When I say *come by* or *lie down* or *away to me*, I want you to shout them at the top of your voice... she'll be your friend for life after that."

After some time, Joe conjured a pair of binoculars from the poacher's pocket of his jacket and scanned the distant slopes. When Lass eventually reappeared, it was as a black dot oscil- lating on the fringe of a dirty-white blob. Expectantly, Tommy waited for his cue, but as the approaching mass slowly materi- alised into individual sheep, Joe crooked a thumb and forefinger between his lips and emitted a series of whistles. Grinning at the boy's obvious disappointment, he laid a reassuring hand on Tommy's shoulder.

"She's still too far off to respond to voice commands; we'll give it a go when she gets closer." A few minutes later, a faint bleating filtered through the air.

"Come by." Joe muttered.

"*Come by!*" Tommy screamed and then stared in amazement, as the collie seemed to freeze in mid-stride, an extended forepaw held at a gravity-defying angle. A shrill blast from Joe sent Lass scuttling away to her left.

"Lie down." Joe prompted.

"*Lie down!*" Tommy's command was greeted as previously; again Joe whistled, causing the dog to disappear from view behind a clump of heather.

"Away to me." Joe breathed as a stubborn ewe made a dash back towards the mountain.

"*Away to me!*" Tommy shrieked and then marvelled as the dog instantly wheeled to her right, cutting off the sheep's escape route.

That evening, after much coaxing from Joe, Tommy agreed to deliver the collie's supper. Fearing the worst, the boy cat-footed his way to the hayshed, the dish of food held protectively before him. Much to his surprise, Lass greeted his arrival with a bout of tail wagging and then, flopping onto her belly, squirmed towards him. Overcome by the moment, Tommy crouched down and, leaving the food within easy reach, scratched the animal's chin. Whining softly, the collie rolled onto her back, presenting her unprotected belly to the newest superior in her pack. Swaggering back to the farmhouse, Tommy realised that he had just had a day that he would never forget.

Despite Tommy's best efforts, sleep engulfed him long before the broad shoulders of Slieveduff robbed the gold from the windows on the west-facing slopes of Coom Beama. Next morning, Eileen seemed even more grumpy than usual.

"*Phwitt.*" She kept repeating, mopping her glistening brow. "*It's rotten, there isn't a puff... phwitt.*" After a breakfast of boiled egg and soda bread, Tommy escaped to the yard and was instantly taken by the colour of the sky above the mountain. Instead of the cloudless blue of previous days, it seemed to have darkened to an opaque navy, except for some bright splashes at either side of the peak.

Out of the corner of his eye, Tommy glimpsed Lass scurry towards the hayshed. Her demeanour was not that of the industrious canine of yesterday but was more akin to the cowering creature of old. Tommy called to the collie but, not receiving a response, started off in her wake. Quivering in her favourite corner, Lass whined softly at the boy's approach. Then, as the terrified animal seemed to shrink before his eyes, Tommy heard the rumble of distant thunder.

Back in the yard, Tommy stared disbelievingly to the west. No longer was there a mountain, just a solid veil of dense purple that stretched from the bluish tinge of the upper meadow to the fathomless black of the sky. For a moment his thoughts turned to the sheep on the mountain, to the lambs... how would they find their mothers through such a blanket of cloud? His train of thought was derailed as the world suddenly lit up and, just as the first huge drops began to fall, there was an ear-splitting crash, quickly followed by several lesser explosions. As an acrid odour permeated the air, the boy sprinted back to the safety of the farmhouse and the familiar strangeness of his extended family.

After about twenty minutes, whether due to Joe's profane outbursts or Eileen's constant praying, the thunder abated. The downpour continued for almost another hour before the first glimmer of light appeared above the crown of the mountain.

To celebrate her triumph over the elements, Eileen brewed a pot of tea and produced a shop-bought cake – a rare treat in the farmhouse. Afterwards, Tommy donned his windcheater and wellingtons to join Joe and Lass on an inspection tour of the livestock.

"The snails are very high." Joe remarked, returning past the outbuildings. "Look, that fella is nearly up to the roof. That's a sure sign of more rain; there'll be no hay cut for a while yet."

"With the help of God it'll clear before *St. Swithin's.*" Eileen said, crossing herself as Joe stooped to untie his boots.

Bored with the unusual lack of activity about the farmyard, Tommy found his attention drawn to the roar from the overflowing stream by the eastern boundary of the property. Following the torrent downhill, he could see that the lake had become expanding brown eddy. Fascinated, he hastened his steps until a disembodied voice halted him in his tracks.

"Who are you?" The voice repeated. Tommy turned to face a lad of about his own age, attired in a green windcheater, jeans and wellingtons. "What are you doing here?" The stranger asked in a television accent.

"I'm Tommy, my aunt and uncle live in the last house up the hill. I'm..."

"You're Helen Casey's lad?" It was more statement than question. Tommy nodded and took a hesitant step forward. "I'm Shane, I'm from Dublin but I've come to my granny Donovan's for my holidays. Where are you from?"

"Town."

"What town?"

"Shrutraw, back over there..." Tommy pointed past Coom Beama.

"That little place? That's not a town; that's a street, hah." Shane turned away dismissively.

"Are you fishing?" Tommy asked, ignoring the jibe.

"No point fishing today: the water is still rising. Maybe tomorrow, or the day after..."

"Oh..." Tommy's disappointment was palpable.

"Hey, I know something we could do: it's a two man job... are you man enough?"

After supper, Eileen surprised Tommy by drawing him towards her and whispering conspiratorially.

"He's polishing his shoes; you'd better sleep in my bed tonight." Holding a silencing finger to her lips, she straightened and began to clear the table. A few minutes later, Joe emerged from his bedroom wearing his second-best tweed jacket, tan trousers and his brown Sunday shoes.

"Can we go fishing tomorrow?" Tommy called as Joe dipped his middle finger in the holy water font by the front door.

"We'll see..." Joe grunted before lowering the peak of his cap against the weak evening sunlight. Eileen muttered something about *'Holy Mother of God'*, and withdrew to complete the washing-up. Tommy seized his opportunity to liberate the binoculars from Joe's jacket and hurried up to his room.

Standing at the gable window, Tommy gasped at how close Coom Beama had become through the powerful lenses of Joe's spyglasses. Traffic on the pass was light but, while actual registration plates were still a blur, he could now identify the make and model of each car.

Then he saw it, there was no mistake: Mum's *Fiesta*, climbing steadily towards the pass. Even with the benefit of the binoculars, the angle of the ascent made it impossible to determine who was actually in the car... until it levelled momentarily at the summit... Mum was alone. Where had she been... visiting more neighbours? Why had she not called to see her family... her son? To the metallic *ching-ching* of a distressed blackbird, Tommy swallowed the dry lump in his throat and retired to the cold comfort of Eileen's double bed.

It was the snoring that woke Tommy: deep irregular snorts, interspersed with breathless gasps and whining moans. Bemused, Tommy craned his neck to where Joe lay slumped beside the window, naked except for a pair of off-white underpants.

"You can go back to your own room now." Eileen whispered. "Or, if you'd prefer, you can get dressed and have breakfast with me. Just don't make any noise..." She eased from the bed and, pulling on her navy dressing gown, slipped silently from the room.

"Is Joe sick?" Tommy asked, buttering a slice of brown bread.

"I suppose you could call it that!" Eileen sighed after an unusually long pause.

"Is he... going to... to die?" The lump had come back to his throat.

"No, of course not." She forced a scornful laugh.

"But..."

"You wouldn't understand. Now, eat your breakfast before it gets cold."

When Joe still hadn't surfaced by noon, Tommy decided to find his own entertainment. Eileen was adamant that the boy shouldn't fish the lake without adult supervision, so that left him with only one option. Yesterday's adventure had taught Tommy a timely lesson; yesterday, he had been Shane's pawn.

"You keep watch." Shane had ordered, stationing Tommy by the gap in McCarthy's hedge. *"If anyone comes or if you see their dog, just shout 'Grouse, Grouse, Grouse', we can pretend that we're looking for Granda's dog."* Tommy had maintained his vigil for a full twenty minutes, abandoning his post only when he caught a distant glimpse of the Dublin boy jogging towards the bottom of the hill, his jacket bulging with his ill-gotten gains. Today would be different; today, Tommy would do things his way.

Once through the hole in the hedge, the path through the overgrown haggard was easy to find. After a few dozen stealthy steps, Tommy emerged into a little clearing only to find himself faced by McCarthy's Alsatian dog. Open mouthed, Tommy froze in terror. Although the dog lifted his head from the comfort of his forepaws, he showed no signs of hostility.

"Don't move, boy." A male voice cautioned. "Jack, stay!" The voice continued as the undergrowth began to vibrate. "Aha. Who have we here?" A tall man emerged from the foliage, a briar-hook balanced in his hand. "Come, Jack!" The man slapped a thigh; the dog sprang to his feet and, tail wagging, padded forward. "Well, boy, what brought you in here anyway?"

"I was looking for... for... for *Grouse.*" Maybe there was an escape route after all. Crouching to fondle the dog's ears, the man chuckled softly. It looked as though the *Grouse* trick had worked.

"Didn't you get enough gooseberries yesterday?" The man asked, getting to his feet and plucking a few hairy fruits from a scraggly bush. "There's a good crop this year, enough for all of us."

"I've never eaten a gooseberry." Tommy drew courage from the apparent friendliness of the man.

"What about yesterday; don't tell me that your friend ate them all!"

"He's not my friend, 'twas he picked the berries and then ran off home with them."

"Ah, he robbed both of us so! What's your name, boy?" The man asked proffering a handful of berries.

"I'm Tommy... I..." Cautiously, he bit into a red-green fruit.

"Well, Tommy, what would Joe and Eileen say if they knew you were here?" Tommy seemed to give the question some thought.

"I'd be in trouble."

"We won't tell them so." The man chuckled again.

"Do you live here?" Tommy asked, aping Shane's assertiveness.

"Sometimes, but usually I live in America, New York."

"My dad lives in New York." Tommy fidgeted excitedly. "Do you know him?"

"New York is a big place." The man's smile had vanished.

"Is it bigger than Shrutraw?" The man nodded. "Is it bigger than Dublin?" Another nod. "Wow, that's big. Can I go home now, please?"

"Off you go, Tommy. Do you want a few more gooseberries?"

"No thanks, I don't like them." With a final glance at the dozing dog, Tommy spun around and hurried back through the gap in the hedge.

Even as Tommy entered the yard, Joe's voice rang out through the open window.

"He does have rights and so does the child; *he* shouldn't be deprived. His mother was... and that was wrong..."

"Deprived? *She* was deprived? What about me... what...?" Eileen whined.

"That was different, that..."

"Oh yes, it was different all right, it was very..." Scorn added edge to Eileen's tone.

"But isn't that's all the more reason…?"

"*He* has no right to Tommy, he…"

"If *he* doesn't itself, Tommy has every right to *him*. We had parents and, especially because of Helen, Tommy has even more…"

"And what if it happens again and she's saddled with another…?"

"It's their right, if that's what they want!"

"Stop it! I don't want to hear…" She sounded close to tears.

"It's natural… two normal young…"

"Normal, natural? Oh, you're a fine one to talk. What about last night? Where are you going? I'm not finished!"

"I am!" Joe's boots resounded against the flagged floor.

"Where are you going? You're not…"

"I'm only doing what I should have done years ago." Joe exploded from the doorway, scattering the flock of young chickens that hunted for morsels swept from the kitchen floor. Concealed behind the rain barrel at the gable eaves' chute, Tommy watched his uncle march towards the road.

About twenty minutes later, Joe returned in the company of the man from the gooseberry patch.

"Tommy, this is Mike, he's a better fisherman than me. He'll take you to the lake."

"Well, Tommy, what about it?" Mike prompted, conjuring a pair of disassembled rods from behind his back.

"Is it all right? What about Eileen?" Tommy's eyes alternated between the men's faces.

"If it's all right with the two of you, Eileen and me don't matter. Go on, enjoy yourselves!"

It took a while for Tommy to master the spinning rod. After three fruitless hours, Mike suggested that they call it a day and return on the following afternoon. Later, while supper waited on the table, Tommy kept the binoculars trained on Coom Beama until Mum's car disappeared over the crest of the pass.

Next morning, after a gulped breakfast, Tommy renewed his vigil at the gable window and grinned his satisfaction when the green *Fiesta* materialised through the glare of the morning sun.

It was just before noon when Mike called for Tommy and, less than thirty minutes later, he had talked his pupil through the landing of his first fish, a half-pound brown trout. Shortly before six o'clock, Tommy waved goodbye to Mike before presenting Eileen with his haul of six trout. While Eileen prepared the fish for supper, Tommy returned the binoculars to the pocket of Joe's jacket.

After supper, Joe sauntered to the doorway for his customary routine of stretching and burping.

"Ah, yeah." Joe sighed, returning to the table and refilling his mug. "That's not a bad looking sky. I think we could make a start on the hay tomorrow!"

"Thanks be to God!" Eileen said, absently skimming crumbs from the table. About an hour later, the sound of a car engine tore Tommy's attention away from his trawl through Joe's glory hole. Taking the stairs two-at-a-time, he reached the kitchen as his mother crossed the threshold.

"Mum." He squealed, rushing to her open arms. "What are you doing here?"

"I've come to take you home. Gather your things!"

"Did we get a baby?" He eyed her uncertainly.

"A baby? Whatever gave you that idea? A baby indeed, you can't get a baby just... just..." Three pairs of adult eyes dropped to focus on different corners of the room.

Tommy seemed to digest the news for a moment before suddenly brightening and tugging at the sleeve his mother's cardigan.

"Mum, can I stay for another little while, please?" All eyes were now refocused on Tommy. "It'll give you more space... more time... I'll go home when we have the hay saved!"

SUN STRUCK

While the eighth of the eighth, eighty-eight is an easy date to re-member, it's one day that I'd much prefer to forget. That morn-ing, my summer Manhattan bar job was not the reason that I'd boarded the number two subway train at Gun Hill Road station; that morning, I'd intended going all the way to Times Square, to meet Alanna.

I'd been waiting for almost two years, ever since Alanna had spent that summer with her grandmother, at the end of our street. It seemed that Nan Tobin's emigrant daughter had considered her native village a safer vacation environment for a precocious teenager than the bright lights of New York City.

I'd found it hard to believe that Alanna was more than two years my junior. She was tall, almost six-feet in her white *Nike* runners. She had the silky blonde hair of her father's Nordic an-cestors, the deep brown Tobin eyes and, a tan that accentuated the pearliness of her movie-star smile. This exotic creature was a world away from the girls we knew: she wore *John Lennon* sun glasses, sometimes on the crown of her head; she drank draught *Guinness*, with her uncle, in the snug of our pub; she openly smoked duty-free *Marlboro* cigarettes and, her knowl-edge of birth control would bring a pubescent blush to the most worldly in our circle.

On sunny days, she would swim nude in the local lake and, at dusk, the tinkle of her laughter could be heard from behind the bicycle shed of the village primary school. I fell in love at her very first '*Hi*'.

Alanna's presence had triggered an unprecedented testoster-one surge throughout the entire parish. Older lads, who had jobs, money and cars, and who wouldn't be seen dead with a fourteen-year-old, were soon hovering like moths around a flame. As faint hope paled to utter despair, fate threw me an un-likely lifeline. Alanna's duty-free cigarette supply had become exhausted and, while I was still someway short of serious date potential, my access to the pub's stockroom had made me an invaluable ally.

Suddenly, my summer was filled with the aromas of honey-suckle and new-mown hay, the tang of sinful cider from inti-mately shared flagons, and visions of Alanna, illuminated by a halo of dancing fireflies, beckoning from the sunset-bloodied waters around Liberty Island. When Alanna finally returned home, my resultant pain was greatly relieved by the unexpected attentions of the local girls. Apparently, if the sumptuous wild-child had deemed me a worthy companion, I merited a closer look from those nearer home.

Alanna did not return in eighty-seven. All through a second winter, my plan continued to incubate: just as soon as I'd fin-ished my *Leaving Cert*, I would forsake the incestuous parochi-alism of village life for the cosmopolitan anonymity of *The Big Apple*. With Ireland deep in recession, I cajoled my parents into granting me a holiday release on the understanding that, should a university place materialise, I would definitely return.

That's why I'd been riding the subway from The Bronx to 110th Street station for the previous four weeks. By then, I was something of a veteran, but imagine my surprise, on the first morning, to discover that I was the only white person in the entire car. My relief must have shown when an equally pale face boarded at Allenton Avenue. He was a spidery little man with a huge aquiline nose and glasses with milk-bottle lenses. After a furtive glance, he settled into the seat nearest the door and bent closer to his newspaper.

Over the next few weeks, we shared the car on about a dozen occasions and, although we never quite reached the verbal stage, we sometimes exchanged nods, particularly when I'd sidestep past him at my stop. On the morning of August 8th, *Uncle Sam* – as I had mentally dubbed him – arrived right on cue. At 116th Street, my attention was drawn to a pair of new arrivals. They were big men – white – their ruddy faces partially obscured by large *Elvis*-type sunglasses. Idly, I wondered at their logic in wearing long Macintoshes in such sweltering heat. Sam had noticed them too; he seemed to shrink as they ignored several vacant seats and stood claustrophobically close to his position.

My curiosity swelled to fascination when Sam darted towards the exit at my usual stop, only for the strangers to grab his arms and flank him onto the platform. My heart pounding, I followed. I still had almost two hours before my rendezvous with Alanna and I could already visualise her hanging on to my every word, as I related my account of Sam's abduction. I continued apace until all three veered into a narrow alley.

"I'll get it, I'll..." Sam squawked, his kicking feet not reaching the ground.

That was when I noticed the pistol that was levelled at the base of the captive's skull, its barrel glinting evilly in the brilliant morning sunlight. I ducked back from the mouth of the alley and cannoned into a huge black man in a security guard's uniform.

"Help, they've dragged him into the alley, they have guns. Call 999!" I blurted.

"911!" He corrected, uncoupling a large black device from his trouser-belt; it was my first sight of a mobile telephone.

Fascinated, I watched him thumb the buttons on the face of the contraption and, as he connected, I attempted a step towards the alley only to have my progress halted by his iron grip on my shoulder.

"No way, kid." The giant cautioned. "Go grab a coffee." I found myself being propelled through swing-doors into the air-conditioned cool of a diner.

Amazingly, neither staff nor clientele seemed in the least disturbed by the choruses of sirens that continued to scream for almost thirty minutes. I had just refused a third top-up from a middle-aged waitress with hollow eyes, when I sensed a towering presence at my table.

"The ol' guy bought it... sorry, kid." The security guard turned and left as silently as he had arrived. I tried to rationalise my sense of loss, I hadn't even known the little man's name... his business... his race... and yet, my vision began to blur.

Sometime later, another looming shape interrupted my thoughts... the Macintosh had been discarded but there was no mistaking the man who had held the pistol to Sam's head. I heard him order a coffee and a chocolate doughnut. His accent was London, East end.

I averted my eyes to monitor his reflected movements in a row of advertisement mirrors on the opposite wall. My focus rested on the red rose tattoo on his right forearm; when he turned to leave, his left forearm showed another tattoo: the crossed hammers of *West Ham United Football Club*. Reaching the exit, he suddenly turned, raised his sunshades and peered curiously in my direction. Trying to keep my knees from knocking together, I arose and, feigning nonchalance, strolled towards the door marked *Restrooms*.

Once in the hallway, I rushed through the fire exit to find myself mere yards from the crime scene. I hit the sidewalk running and didn't stop until I'd reached the subway station. The killer had given me more than a second glance; I just couldn't take the risk that he would complete the jigsaw and come looking for me. That was why I broke my first and only date with Alanna... To this day, my ego wants to believe that she did actually turn up, but another part of me shudders at the thought of disappointment clouding the dark sparkle of her defiant eyes.

A week later, with my American dream soured to a recurring nightmare, I scanned my examination results. It was there in black-and-white: university would not be calling. In just seven days, I'd gone from having the world at my feet to having those same feet nailed to the wooden slats behind my parents' bar counter. Ironically, while lack of ambition was partially responsible for my predicament, it also proved my ultimate saviour. Against all expectations, I warmed to the bar business and, within a few years, I had become a virtual pillar of village society.

The mid-nineties saw change in the air. A succession of Government tax amnesties, followed by urban renewal development concessions, triggered a flood of money, from tax evaders and other dubious sources, back from foreign havens to the Irish property market. *The Celtic Tiger* was on the prowl and beginning to prey on the families of those who had sustained the State while others, better connected, had systematically bled it dry.

Nuala was now in my life, a city girl who'd come to teach at the village school. We married in ninety-eight and, after a week's honeymoon in Paris, slipped happily into the gentle tenor of village life.

It took us a further ten years to become airborne again. Now we were four: eight-year-old Sarah and Brian, who was almost six, had completed our family circle. After much deliberation and trawling of the Internet, Nuala decided that the Easter break would be a good time to visit the south of Spain.

Malaga proved the perfect choice: our self-catering apartment was a mere three-minute walk from the beach and adjacent to such a variety of amenities that we instantly agreed to return in the autumn. A couple of Irish children had befriended our pair and, on the third evening of our stay, we happily accepted their parents' invitation to dinner at their villa. To our surprise, it transpired that our hosts, Sharon and Wayne, lived less than an hour's drive from our home and, exchanging telephone numbers, we agreed keep in touch after we'd all returned to Ireland.

"I didn't want to say anything earlier but I don't trust them!" Nuala confided to me after our children had been tucked up in their beds. I tried to counter but – as always – she had the final say. "I grew up beside people like those. How can they afford that lifestyle? What does *in business* mean, anyway? What bloody business?"

I suppose if I hadn't lost Nuala's new digital camera at the airport, I'd probably have never met Wayne again. After a few days of the silent treatment, it dawned on me that Wayne had taken as many photos of us as we had taken of them. In serious need of brownie points, I phoned Wayne and he readily agreed to have a DVD containing every shot that we appeared in, ready for collection on that very evening.

Maybe Nuala is right, I conceded, pressing the intercom buzzer at Wayne's electronically controlled entrance gates.

They must be entertaining. I decided, eyeballing the dozen-or-so top-of-the-range vehicles parked beside the impressive Edwardian house. Parking my Astra, I caught a fleeting glimpse of a dark burly figure dragging a pair of enormous rottweilers back into the shadows by the stable block at the rear of the house.

"If it's a bad time..." I said, gesturing towards the fleet of motors, as Wayne opened the solid teak door.

"No, I'm all alone; they're just... business. Come in!" Wayne grinned, gripping my hand and hauling me through the doorway. Reluctantly, he deferred to my preference for coffee over alcohol and ushered me into a huge lounge, where still images of Wayne's family flickered on a giant plasma TV screen.

Suddenly, there she was; brown eyes taunting, sunglasses perched on the crown of her gorgeous blonde head; her tan a shade deeper but her smile as pearly as ever...

"Alanna!" I gasped, totally oblivious to Wayne's return.

"You know Alanna?" He beamed, handing me a *cappuccino.* "I do business with Harry." He grabbed the remote control and heartlessly thumbed Alanna's face from the screen. An instant later she reappeared... smaller... more distant... there was somebody else...

"There's Harry..." Wayne beamed... but I wasn't listening; instead, I gaped in horror at the brawny forearms that obscured Alanna's bikini top... the tattooed forearms of the man who had stared at me in that 110th Street diner... just minutes after he had murdered *Uncle Sam...*